FLAMES OF THE CROWS BETRAYAL

MIKEL WILSON

Edited by
JACQULYN WARD

Copyright © 2024. All rights reserved. No part of this book may be reproduced in any form without the written consent of the author, except for brief quotes used in reviews.

This is a work of fiction.Any references or similarities to names, characters, places, events, real people, living or dead, places, or real locals are entirely coincidental.

❀ Created with Vellum

SHARED WORLD

THE RED DRAGON SERIES

Enchanted Elemental Empire

Flames of Betrayal

<u>CONTEMPORARY</u>

Something for Susan

Shattered But not Easily Broken

Picking up the Shattered Pieces

YA/NA FANTASY

ASCENSION OF THE BLOOD THRONE

A Light Beyond the Darkness

A Fallen Kingdom

A Last Glimmer of Hope

<u>SHARED WORLD</u>

Orphans Revenge

Tears of an Orphan

Ground of Blood

Darkest of Days

SHARED WORLD/ ROMCOM
ASSASINATION UNIVERSITY

Campus Flings and Killer Instincts
Campus Kills and Cold Vengeance
Sweethearts and Blow Darts
Twas the Fight Before Christmas

FOLLOW ME

ON YOUR FAVORITE SOCIAL
MEDIA SITES
Authormikelwilson.net
Facebook
TikTok
Instagram
FB Readers Group

I am truly blessed to say that I have gone through betrayal and without it, I wouldn't be the man I am today. If you are holding onto any hurts caused by this, LET IT GO. It is only hurting you, sending you good vibes and hope you find healing for your heart.

PROLOGUE

NATALIE

The night air clung to my skin like a second layer, saturated with tension and the taste of rain. I sprinted down the slick street, the chill wind biting into my bones as it whipped through my jacket. Each step reverberated in my ears, a relentless drumbeat amplified by the adrenaline surging through my veins. The city lights blurred in my periphery, a kaleidoscope of colors swirling as I focused solely on the figure ahead—the perp.

"Stop!" I yelled, my voice slicing through the night like a knife. He turned, his eyes wide with panic, and in that instant, I saw the glint of metal. My heart dropped as time slowed; the world shrank to a singular point—the gun he was raising. Instinct kicked in, and I ducked, feeling the rush of wind as a bullet whizzed past my head. The sharp crack of gunfire echoed in my ears, mingling with the roar of my heartbeat.

"Fischer!" My partner, Marcus, shouted from behind me.

A surge of relief washed over me as he intercepted the fleeing suspect, blocking his escape with a commanding presence that only he could master. "Give it up!" he called, his voice steady, as if he were simply asking for a favor rather than confronting a desperate criminal.

For a moment, it seemed like the chaos might end there. The perp hesitated, and a smile crept onto Marcus's face as he turned to me. "We got him!"

But then everything changed in an instant. The suspect's fear morphed into raw desperation, and he swung back around, the gun raised once more. My heart stopped, frozen in horror as I watched Marcus's smile fade. The crack of the gunshot rang out again, louder this time—a sickening sound that reverberated through the alley.

"No!" I screamed, instinctively pulling my weapon and firing at the criminal. My aim was steady despite the chaos; the bullet found its mark, and the suspect collapsed, his body crumpling to the ground like a discarded rag doll. I stood over him, breath heavy in my chest, adrenaline still coursing through my veins as I kicked the gun away.

But my focus shifted instantly to Marcus. He was on the ground, coughing, blood pooling beneath him. "Officer down!" I shouted into my radio, panic rising as I knelt beside him. "This is Detective Natalie Fischer. My partner's been shot!"

"Nat, I'm okay," he gasped, his voice strained but somehow still trying to reassure me. I could see the blood seeping through his uniform, the crimson against the blue stark and horrifying. "I barely feel anything," he managed a choked laugh, but it was hollow, a weak attempt to lighten the gravity of the moment.

"Just a flesh wound," he said, but the sound twisted in my gut. I glanced down, my stomach lurching as the reality crashed over me. Blood was pooling beneath him, dark and menacing, like the shadows of the alley that encased us.

"Be quiet! We have an ambulance on the way. It's okay," I urged, my voice trembling as I pressed my hands against the wound, desperate to staunch the flow of blood.

"Hey, Natalie," he rasped, his eyes flickering with a light that I desperately wished would remain. "Do you remember when we were at the academy together and everyone thought—"

His words faded, the breath leaving his body in a slow, agonizing silence. The light in his eyes dimmed, and I shook him, panic igniting in my chest. "Marcus! Marcus, don't you dare do this to me!"

But he was still, his body growing heavier in my grasp, the warmth of his blood soaking through my fingers. The sirens wailed in the distance, but they felt like they were fading into a void, the sound swallowed by the over-whelming silence that enveloped me. The world around me became a blur; the screams of the crowd, the chaos of the gunfire, all dulled to a haunting quiet.

I was lost in that moment, a stillness that felt like eternity as I shook him, desperate for a response. "Marcus!" I cried, my voice breaking. The sound echoed in the alley, a haunting lament that mocked my denial.

The paramedics arrived, but they were mere shadows in the periphery of my vision. I couldn't hear them; the sound had left my ears, leaving me in a deafening void. The urgency of their movements felt distant, like watching a scene unfold in a dream, one where I was trapped in a nightmare with no escape.

The wind picked up, howling through the alley, carrying the weight of my despair. It tugged at my hair, whipped around my face, but I barely felt it. All I could focus on was

Marcus, the warmth slipping away from him, the life extinguishing before my eyes.

"Stay with me! Please, stay with me!" I pleaded, my heart pounding like a wild animal trapped in a cage. I could feel the sharp sting of tears in my eyes, blurring my vision, but I fought against them, refusing to let despair claim me.

The paramedics rushed to Marcus, their voices urgent and commanding, but I was lost in my own world, the reality of his condition crashing down around me. I could see the panic in their eyes as they worked to stabilize him, but their movements felt like a slow-motion film, each second stretching into eternity.

As they lifted him onto a stretcher, desperation surged within me. "No! Don't take him away from me!" My voice broke, raw and guttural as I reached for him, my fingers grazing his hand, cold and lifeless.

"Detective Fischer, we need you to step back," one of the medics said, his voice firm but compassionate.

But I couldn't move. I was rooted to the spot, the weight of my grief pinning me down. "I can't... I can't lose him. Not like this," I whispered, my breath hitching in my throat.

As they loaded him into the ambulance, the wind whipped around me again, colder this time, as if it were mourning with me. The alley was filled with flashing lights and the muted sounds of chaos, but all I could hear was the deafening silence of loss echoing in my mind.

"Stay with me, Marcus," I whispered into the night, the words feeling like a prayer, a plea to the universe to bring him back, to undo the horror that had just unfolded. But the wind carried my words away, leaving only a chilling emptiness behind.

As the ambulance doors slammed shut, the reality of what had happened crashed over me like a wave, pulling me under.

I stumbled back against the cool, damp wall of the alley, my heart in freefall. This wasn't how it was supposed to end.

With the weight of grief settling heavily on my shoulders, I turned my gaze to the sky, where dark clouds loomed ominously overhead. I felt the wind pick up again, this time as if it were urging me to move, to fight, to not let his sacrifice be in vain.

With a deep breath, I wiped away the tears that had begun to fall, the chill of the air stinging my cheeks. I felt a flicker igniting within me, a burning ember in the cold void of despair.

"Not like this,"

CHAPTER 1

NATALIE

"*N*atalie!" A voice screamed bringing me Out of the darkness. The light slowly peaked through allowing me to see clearly. The sound of her bell signaling that the session was nearly over.

I BLINKED TWICE, trying to shake off the weight of my memories, the oppressive shadow of that alley creeping back into my mind. The familiar surroundings of Dr. Alicia Hayes office began to settle in, offering a worn but comforting refuge from my tumultuous thoughts. The walls were a deep burgundy, a rich color that wrapped around me like a warm embrace. It was a color that felt both regal and soothing, a stark contrast to the chaos that often swirled within me. The light reflected off the polished wood floor, casting a warm glow that danced along the edges of the room, breaking the somber ambiance just enough to remind me that I was safe here.

THE OFFICE WAS a blend of professionalism and warmth, a carefully curated space where vulnerability was welcomed. Bookshelves lined one wall, filled with texts on psychology, criminology, and even a few novels that hinted at Dr. Alicia's own interests. A potted fern sat on the window sill, its leaves lush and green, adding a touch of life to the otherwise subdued decor. The window, framed in dark wood, offered a view of world outside, a bustling street that felt a million miles away from the heavy silence within these four walls.

DR. ALICIA WAS SEATED across from me, her presence steadying in the wake of my stormy emotions. She had been my therapist ever since my mother left me at the age of fifteen. She was always there for me even when I didn't want her to be. She felt more like family than a therapist, she wore her signature black-framed glasses, which perched slightly down her nose, giving her an air of both authority and approachability. Her pleated skirt swayed gently as she shifted in her chair, her posture relaxed yet attentive. The graying strands of her hair framed her face, a testament to the years she had spent listening to the anguished stories of others, guiding them through their darkest moments.

"DR. ALICIA," I murmured, my voice barely a whisper. I could feel the weight of the past pressing against my chest, the memories of Marcus's death threatening to overwhelm me once more.

. . .

"Yes, Natalie," she replied, her voice calm and measured, a soothing balm to my frayed nerves. "You need to dissociate yourself from what happened in that alley. You need to work on dealing with that loss."

Her words hung in the air, heavy with meaning. I had been here countless times before, yet each session felt like treading water in a vast ocean of grief. I glanced down at my phone, the sudden buzz pulling me back to reality. The screen illuminated my face, a stark reminder of my responsibilities outside this room. It was a text from the captain.

Well, duty calls. Same time next week?

I hesitated, my fingers hovering over the screen. The weight of my badge felt heavier than ever, a constant reminder of the life I had chosen—a life where I was trained to protect, to serve, and yet I had failed to save the one person who mattered most. I looked back at Dr. Alicia, her expression a mix of concern and encouragement.

Dr. Alicia had been my therapist for as long as I could remember ever since I was a dumb kid. But since that fateful night when Marcus had been needlessly shot down in the line of duty I had been seeing her more regular. Her approach was gentle yet firm, a delicate balance that was often necessary to navigate the choppy waters of my grief. I admired her ability to maintain her composure, her warm smile a constant in an ever-changing world. She had a way of

MIKEL WILSON

making me feel safe, *even when I was drowning in the depths of my despair.*

"Do you want to take a moment?" she asked, reading the turmoil in my eyes. The way her brow furrowed slightly showed her genuine concern, a reminder that she was not just a therapist, but a person who cared about my well-being.

I nodded, the lump in my throat making it hard to speak. I took a deep breath, inhaling the faint scent of lavender that lingered in the room. It was a calming aroma, one that reminded me of late nights spent pouring over case files, the scent of lavender candles flickering in the background as I tried to drown out the memories of that night.

The silence stretched between us, a fragile thread that held my fragmented thoughts at bay. I could hear the faint ticking of the clock on the wall, each tick a reminder of time passing—time that I wished I could reclaim, time that had stolen Marcus from me.

Dr. Alicia looked at me, her eyes showing exactly what I felt, a sense of being lost. Dr

Alicia knew me better than I knew myself, I often thought. Sometimes I felt like she could see right through me to my heart and read my innermost thoughts. *Losing Marcus over a year ago and watching him be shot down haunted my nightmares, but I would never allow myself to put my guard down. Any perp that made any movement towards me would be put down. No flag would be draped over my casket- at least, not anytime soon.*

FLAMES OF THE CROWS BETRAYAL

. . .

I WALKED down the busy station, the smells of stale coffee filling the air as I made my way down the hall. I took a deep breath; I knew this talk with the captain was not going to be good. The fluorescent lights overhead buzzed softly, their harsh glare reflecting off the polished tiles of the floor, creating a sterile atmosphere that felt more like a hospital than a place meant to uphold justice.

THE POLICE STATION, bustling with activity, was a cacophony of voices, ringing phones, and the occasional clatter of paperwork being shuffled around. Officers hurried past me, their faces a mix of determination and fatigue. Some exchanged banter while others rushed by with a sense of urgency that made me feel even smaller and more anxious. I could hear snippets of conversations about ongoing cases, the latest leads, and the mundane details of their daily lives. I felt like an intruder in their world, a lone figure lost in the sea of blue uniforms and the weight of responsibility that hung thick in the air.

I GLANCED at the bulletin board plastered with notices about community events, missing persons, and upcoming training sessions. A few flyers were hastily pinned up, some faded and crumpled from being tacked and re-tacked too many times. The board seemed to reflect the chaos and urgency of our work—always changing, always filled with reminders of the lives we were here to protect and serve. But it also served as a constant reminder of the burden we carried, the weight of the lives lost and the cases unsolved.

. . .

MIKEL WILSON

As I walked, my heart raced, each step feeling heavier than the last. I had rehearsed this conversation a hundred times in my head, imagining every possible outcome. Would it be a simple chat, or would it end in reprimands and disappointment? The thought of facing Captain Howard made my palms sweat. He was a no-nonsense leader, a man known for his sharp tongue and unwavering commitment to the law. I respected him deeply, but that didn't alleviate my anxiety.

I turned a corner and caught sight of the captain's office door—solid oak with a brass nameplate that read "Captain John Howard." It was a door that felt impenetrable, a barrier between my apprehension and whatever awaited me on the other side. I hesitated, my feet rooted to the ground as I took a moment to collect myself. The world outside the station faded away, replaced by the whirlwind of thoughts swirling in my mind.

What if he was disappointed in me? What if I had let my team down? The weight of expectation pressed down on my chest. I had been with the department long enough to know that mistakes were part of the job, but that didn't mean they were easy to accept. I had always prided myself on my ability to handle difficult situations, but this was different. This was the captain—he had a way of making every conversation feel like a performance review, every word dissected and analyzed.

Taking a deep breath, I finally mustered the courage to approach the door. My hand hovered over the brass knob, hesitating for just a moment before I knocked lightly. The

FLAMES OF THE CROWS BETRAYAL

sound echoed in the silence, a stark contrast to the noise of the station. I could hear movement inside, the rustling of papers and the faint sound of a chair scraping against the floor. A moment later, I heard a deep voice call out, "Come in."

I PUSHED THE DOOR OPEN, the hinges creaking slightly as I stepped inside. The office was a reflection of the captain himself—orderly yet imposing. Bookshelves lined the walls, filled with law enforcement manuals, case files, and a few personal mementos that hinted at his life outside the police force.

THE CAPTAIN'S office sat at the very end of the dimly lit corridor, its door a plain, unassuming slab of wood, worn and scuffed from years of use. The brass doorknob glinted faintly in the flickering fluorescent lights overhead. The air inside was thick with the scent of stale coffee, mingling with the faint aroma of old paper and leather—a mix that spoke of long hours spent weighing decisions that could turn lives upside down.

THE AIR FELT CHARGED with authority, and I suddenly felt like a student summoned to the principal's office.

CHAPTER 2

NATALIE

*C*aptain Howard's desk was a fortress of paperwork and clutter, a testament to the chaotic nature of his work. Stacks of files teetered precariously on the edge, while a battered computer hummed quietly, displaying a sea of spreadsheets and reports. The walls were lined with framed commendations and photographs of the captain with various dignitaries, interspersed with a few personal touches—a family photo of his wife and two kids, a faded picture of his college football team, and a weathered plaque that read, "Integrity First."

Captain Howard himself was a man of presence, despite his graying hair and the thinning crown that revealed more scalp than strands. He was in his late fifties, but the lines on his face spoke of a lifetime spent in service, of nights spent on the streets, and of the burdens he carried. His eyes, a deep-set blue, held a flicker of warmth, but they were often clouded with the stress of the job. He wore a crisp blue uniform that seemed to fit him well enough, although the fabric had begun to show signs of wear, just like its occupant.

I stood in front of his desk, feeling the weight of his gaze as he leaned back in his chair. His fingers steepled, a gesture I had come to recognize as a prelude to a lecture. "You wanted to see me, Captain?" I asked, trying to keep my voice steady despite the knot forming in my stomach.

"Sit down, detective." His tone was firm but not unkind. I took a seat in the chair opposite him, its leather cracked and worn from years of use. The chair creaked beneath me, and I felt the tension in the air thicken as he began to speak.

"I received a report about your recent arrest," he said, his voice measured. "I need to talk to you about excessive use of force."

I felt my heart race. "Excessive use of force? Captain, I was just doing my job. The guy punched me in the face! He was a danger to that woman!"

Howard sighed, rubbing his temples as if he were trying to massage away the stress. "I understand that, but breaking his arm? That's not how we do things here. We're supposed to uphold the law, not become vigilantes. I get it you're fiery and have dealt with alot but we have to follow everything by the book."

"I didn't have a choice!" I shot back, my voice rising slightly. "He was attacking me, and I had to protect myself and that woman. He was a criminal! He deserved what he got!"

The captain's expression hardened, and I could see the flicker of disappointment in his eyes. "You're not a rookie. You should know better than to let your emotions cloud your judgment. You're being called into Internal Affairs for this."

"Internal Affairs?" My voice cracked slightly. "You can't be serious! They'll make me out to be some kind of monster!"

"Don't take it personally," he said, his voice softening as he leaned forward, elbows resting on the desk. "They have a job to do, and so do we. It's not about you being a monster; it's about accountability. We have to show the community that we are working toward justice, not revenge."

I felt a swell of frustration. "But Captain, you know me! You know I care about what I do. I was trying to protect that woman, to stop a criminal! How can you not see that?"

"I see that, but you have to understand the bigger picture," he countered, his voice still steady. "We can't afford to let emotions drive our actions. It sets a dangerous precedent."

"Dangerous?" I scoffed. "What's dangerous is letting criminals think they can get away with anything! If I hadn't taken action, who knows what that guy would have done next?"

"Maybe, but there are protocols in place for a reason," he said, his voice rising slightly. "And right now, you're risking your career over this."

"Risking my career?" I echoed incredulously. "I'm risking my life every day out there! And when I finally do something to protect myself and others, I get dragged into Internal Affairs like I'm the bad guy?"

The tension in the room thickened, both of us caught in our convictions, voices rising as emotions flared. "You think this is easy for me?" he shot back, his expression hardening. "I've been in this line of work long enough to know the consequences of letting anger dictate your actions. I have to ensure that you don't spiral down a path that could ruin your life!"

I sat back, feeling the anger simmer beneath the surface. "You think I want to be in this position? You think I enjoy being reprimanded for trying to do my job? You don't understand how it feels out there, Captain. It's not just paperwork and reports!"

He leaned back in his chair, the frustration evident on his face. "And you don't understand the responsibility that comes with this badge. If we let personal feelings dictate our actions, we lose the respect of the community. We lose everything we've worked for."

"Respect?" I scoffed. "What about respect for the victims? For the ones who suffer while we sit here and talk about protocol? We're supposed to protect them!"

"We are," he replied, his voice now low and steady. "But we also have to protect ourselves and our integrity. We can't afford to become what we're fighting against."

Silence hung between us, heavy and charged. I could see the concern etched into his features, a mixture of worry and disappointment. He cared; I knew that. But at that moment, his understanding felt out of reach, like a distant shore I couldn't navigate to.

"Captain," I finally said, my voice quieter, the anger ebbing away, replaced by a sense of resignation. "I just wish you could see it from my perspective. I'm out there every day, facing threats, and trying to keep people safe. It's hard to think about protocols when your life's on the line."

"I do understand, believe me," he said, his gaze softening. "But your safety and the integrity of the department are my priorities. I don't want to see you hurt, and I don't want to see you lose everything you've worked for because of a moment of anger."

I looked down at my hands, feeling the weight of his words. "I just don't think it's fair," I said softly. "I try to do the right thing, but it feels like I'm being punished for it."

"It's not about punishment; it's about growth," he replied gently. "I wouldn't be doing my job if I didn't hold you accountable. It's my responsibility to help you become a better officer."

I looked up, meeting his gaze. In that moment, I saw the concern and care he held for me, deep beneath the frustration and the rules. "I appreciate that, Captain. I really do. I just wish there was a way to make you understand how hard it is out there."

"I know," he said, his voice softening again. "And I want to help you, but you have to meet me halfway. You have to be willing to learn and adjust, even when it's tough."

I nodded slowly, feeling the tension begin to dissipate. "I'll try," I said, the words feeling heavy on my tongue. "But it's going to take time."

"It always does," he replied, a faint smile breaking through the tension. "But we'll figure it out together. I'm here to support you, even when it feels like the world is against you."

I took a deep breath, feeling a flicker of hope amidst the frustration. "Thanks, Captain. I just want to do my job right."

"And you will," he assured, his voice filled with conviction. "Just remember, it's a marathon, not a sprint. We'll get through this together, one step at a time."

As I stood up to leave, I felt a renewed sense of determination. The captain may not fully understand my feelings, but his support gave me the strength to keep fighting for what I believed in. And in that moment, I knew I wouldn't let this setback define who I was as an officer. I would learn, I would grow, and I would continue to protect those who couldn't protect themselves—because that's what it meant to be a cop.

As I walked out of his office, I glanced back at him, and for the first time that day, I felt a sense of understanding between us, a bridge built over the chasm of our differing perspectives. We were on the same team, after all, even if our paths sometimes diverged. And for now, that was enough.

I slammed my papers onto my desk, the sound echoing in the quiet aftermath of my frustration. The station felt like a pressure cooker, and I was the boiling point. I stormed out, my emotions swirling like a tempest in my chest. *Screw this crap. I needed to escape this place.*

CHAPTER 3

NATALIE

The air outside was thick with the scent of asphalt warmed by the sun, mingled with the bitter tang of exhaust fumes. My skin prickled with heat as I made my way to my car, the weight of the day still heavy on my shoulders. Climbing into the driver's seat, I took a moment to breathe, reminding myself to let it go. I cranked up the music, the pulsing beat reverberating through the vehicle, a desperate attempt to drown out the chaos swirling in my mind.

I ACCELERATED the gas pedal and I had become one in the same. I watched the signs whiz by as I beat each light before I quickly merged onto the freeway, hoping to beat the rush hour traffic but I was too late, the line of cars in front of me brought me back to reality and hit me like a brick wall. Traffic was at a standstill, a sea of red brake lights stretching out before me like a wounded serpent. I could feel my irritation mounting, the rhythm of the music clashing with the rhythm of my anger. I leaned on the horn, the sound piercing through the cacophony of frustrated drivers, but it was a futile gesture. Cars were gridlocked, and no one was moving.

I SAT THERE, the heat of the day pressed down like a weight on my shoulders, my palms began to sweat. I glanced around at the other drivers, their faces a mixture of annoyance and resignation. Some were fidgeting with their phones, others looked exasperated, and a few had already resigned themselves to the chaos, leaning back in their seats with a defeated sigh. I felt a flicker of camaraderie with them, but my frustration was still boiling just beneath the surface. I began to honk my horn in frustration

WHEN THE TRUCK door in front of me flung open— a man got out his face twisted in anger. He exited his vehicle, a baseball bat in hand,
my heart dropped. "What is he doing?" I muttered, my instincts kicking in. Adrenaline surged through my veins as I grabbed my service weapon from the holster, my mind racing with the potential consequences of this reckless situation.

HE APPROACHED MY CAR, bat raised, and I quickly stepped out to meet him, gun drawn at his face, the weight of authority heavy in my grip. "I'm detective Fischer of the Oklahoma City Police Department!" I shouted, my voice cutting through the tension in the air.

. . .

MIKEL WILSON

"You came at me to cause bodily harm. I could shoot you right now! Big man getting out of his car in rush hour with a bat only to find himself staring down the barrel of a 40 caliber with a pissed off detective. I cocked my pistol and gripped it tightly, his eyes widened in fear while I took a step towards him.

"Oh seems I have your attention now, I take it you have never been shot? Felt the hot lead pierce your soft skin? Want to make a move? Because I will gladly be your huckleberry." I chuckled.

The world around us seemed to blur as I focused on the man, his eyes widening in fear. The chaos of the traffic jam faded into the background, replaced by the adrenaline coursing through my veins. I could hear the rumble of engines, the honking of horns—people were rolling down their windows, pulling out their cell phones to record the scene unfolding in front of them. A part of me was acutely aware of the cameras capturing every moment, every word, every breath.

"Lower your bat and get back in your truck before I bust you and take your sorry butt downtown,but if you make one sudden move I will end you." I yelled forcefully, my voice firm and unwavering.

"Now do you want to go to jail or wait in this god- awful traffic like everyone else?"

· · ·

FLAMES OF THE CROWS BETRAYAL

HIS HANDS TREMBLED as he slowly lowered the bat dropping it on the steaming asphalt , the anger draining from his face, replaced by a palpable fear. "Okay, okay," he stuttered, glancing nervously around at the crowd forming behind me. I could feel their eyes on us, the weight of judgment hanging in the air. The world had shifted, and suddenly, I was the focal point of a drama playing out in real-time, the hero in a story that could just as easily have turned tragic.

"PICK UP YOUR BAT NOW, and get your butt back in your vehicle." I yelled again.

WITH A SHAKY BREATH, he picked up the bat and retreated to his truck, sliding into the cab with a look of defeat. The crowd erupted in applause, a wave of relief washing over them as the tension dissipated. I felt a mix of pride and anger, my heart still racing from the confrontation. I wanted to scream, to let the chaos of the day pour out of me. But as I climbed back into my car, I could feel the adrenaline ebbing away, leaving only the sharp edge of frustration behind.

FINALLY, the traffic began to move again, a slow trickle that gradually transformed into a steady stream. I navigated through the maze of vehicles, my mind still racing. The chaos of the street seemed to fade as the city began to breathe again, but my thoughts were still a tempest. I needed to calm down.

AS I PULLED into the parking lot of my apartment complex, the familiar sights of home enveloped me like a warm

MIKEL WILSON

embrace. The sun was beginning to set, casting a golden hue over the buildings, and I could smell the rich aroma of freshly cooked food wafting up from the ground floor. My stomach growled in response, reminding me that I hadn't eaten since breakfast.

I PARKED my car and took a deep breath, the familiar scent of my neighborhood flooding my senses. I stepped out, the weight of my service weapon feeling lighter now that I was away from the chaos of the city. The sounds of laughter and chatter drifted up from nearby apartments, and I could hear the sizzling of something delicious being cooked on a grill. My heart began to lighten as I walked towards my door.

AFTER WHAT SEEMED like an eternity I entered my apartment, I was greeted by the comforting warmth of the space. Dominic, my boyfriend, stood in the kitchen, his back to me as he stirred something in a pot. He was freshly promoted to detective, and even though we both carried the weight of our jobs, there was an ease about our home life that I cherished. The kitchen was filled with the aroma of garlic and herbs, a symphony of scents that made my heart swell.

"HEY, BABE!" Dominic called over his shoulder, his voice smooth and inviting. He turned, a smile spreading across his face, and the sight of him instantly melted away the frustration of the day. His bald head and glistening brown skin could make a girl go weak at the knees. After the day I had, he wore a fitted black t-shirt that accentuated his athletic build. "How was your day?"

· · ·

I LEANED AGAINST THE DOORFRAME, taking a moment to soak in the comfort of home. "Oh, you know—just another day in paradise," I replied, forcing a laugh. I could see the concern flicker across his face, and I knew he could sense the tension still lingering in my posture.

DOMINIC CROSSED the small kitchen and wrapped his arms around me, pulling me into a warm embrace. "You look like you've had a rough one," he murmured, his voice low and soothing. I buried my face in his shoulder, inhaling the familiar scent of his cologne mixed with the aroma of the food. It was grounding, a reminder that amidst the chaos outside, I had a sanctuary here.

"I HAD a little run-in with a guy who thought he could take on the world with a bat," I confessed, pulling back slightly to meet his gaze. The warmth in his eyes was comforting, a safe harbor in the storm of my day.

DOMINIC RAISED AN EYEBROW, concern etched on his features. "You didn't get hurt, did you?"

"No, no," I assured him, waving my hand dismissively. "I handled it. But it was just one of those days, you know?"

"TELL me about it while I finish up dinner," he said, turning back to the stove. He began to plate the food, and I could see the vibrant colors of the sautéed vegetables and the perfectly

MIKEL WILSON

cooked chicken glistening on the plates. I felt my stomach rumble again, this time in anticipation.

I TOOK a seat at the small dining table, the familiar wooden surface smooth beneath my fingertips. "It's just been a long week, and today was the icing on the cake. I had a meeting with Internal Affairs, and then that whole debacle with the guy in traffic—" I sighed, running a hand through my hair. "Sometimes it feels like we're fighting an uphill battle."

DOMINIC PLACED a plate in front of me, the steam rising from the food creating a fragrant cloud that enveloped the table. "Yeah, I get that," he said, taking a seat across from me. "But you know what? You're doing an amazing job. You put yourself out there every day, and that takes guts."

I MET HIS GAZE, the sincerity in his voice wrapping around me like a warm blanket. "Thanks, Dom. That means a lot coming from you. I just wish it didn't feel like we're constantly on the edge."

"TRUST ME, I KNOW," he said, his expression thoughtful as he took a bite of the food. "But we have to remember why we do this. We're making a difference, one case at a time."

"YEAH, I KNOW," I replied, taking a forkful of the delicious food. The flavors burst in my mouth, a perfect blend of spices and seasonings that made me close my eyes in bliss. "This is amazing, by the way."

"THANKS! I wanted to cook something special for you," he said, his smile widening. "Figured you could use some comfort food after today."

As WE ATE, the conversation flowed easily between us. We shared stories about our days, the frustrations and triumphs, the moments that made us laugh, and the ones that made us cringe. The weight of the day began to lift, replaced by the warmth of shared laughter and the delicious food that filled our bellies.

AFTER DINNER, we moved to the living room, collapsing onto the couch together, the soft fabric welcoming us like a well-worn embrace. I tucked my legs beneath me, resting my head against his shoulder as we turned on the television. The familiar flicker of the screen illuminated the room, and for a moment, the outside world faded away.

DOMINIC WRAPPED his arm around me, pulling me closer. I could feel the tension in my body slowly dissipating, the chaos of the day replaced by the comfort of our shared space. It was in these moments, amid the laughter and the warmth of his presence, that I found solace. I knew that no matter how chaotic the world outside became, we had each other, and that made everything feel a little more manageable.

As WE SETTLED IN, the sounds of the city outside began to fade, replaced by the gentle hum of our lives. The smell of

MIKEL WILSON

fresh food still lingered in the air, a reminder of the comfort we created together. I felt at peace, knowing that despite the chaos that sometimes surrounded us, I had found my home in Dominic—a place where I could always let my guard down and simply be. And as the television flickered, casting soft shadows across the room, I realized that this was all I needed to recharge and prepare to face the world again. "Hey baby,

"Yes my love." he said with a small smile.

"Congratulations on being promoted to detective. Whoever they pair you with will be a lucky person to have someone as kind as you watching their back."

He bent down and gently kissed the top of my head making my body melt. I slowly looked into his eyes when his lips pressed against mine, making the world around us dissipate into nothingness.

CHAPTER 4

NATALIE

After a night like that with Dom, I felt as if I could take on the world. The warmth of the shared moments lingered in my mind, wrapping around me like a comforting blanket as I stretched and yawned in my empty bed. The sunlight streamed through the curtains, casting gentle rays across the room, but the absence of Dom felt palpable. He had left for work early, and I was still floating in that blissful haze of sleep and contentment. Just a few more minutes, I thought, sinking back into the pillows.

But my reverie was abruptly shattered by the shrill ring of my phone. I groaned and fumbled for it, squinting at the screen.

"Hello?" I answered, my voice thick with sleep.

"Detective, we need you here now. It's a homicide. We're sending you the location."

The words hit me like a splash of cold water. My heart raced as adrenaline surged through my veins. "Great!" I

MIKEL WILSON

replied, instantly alert. I jumped up and threw on some clothes—a pair of jeans and a fitted jacket—before rushing out the door.

The GPS guided me through the winding streets of the city, my mind racing with thoughts of what awaited me. Every stoplight felt like an eternity, each second ticking by as I anticipated the scene. The coordinates led me to an old gas station, its faded sign barely illuminated in the early morning light. I could see police cars lining the entrance, blue and red lights flashing, casting eerie shadows on the cracked pavement.

As I pulled up, a wave of frustration welled up inside me. "This is great, can you move?" I honked my horn, the sound echoing through the stillness of the morning. When the officers finally let me through, I exited my car, the heavy scent of burnt rubber and gasoline hitting me like a punch to the gut.

The gas station was a relic of a bygone era. Its once-bright colors had faded into dull pastels, the paint peeling and the windows clouded with grime. Rust crept along the edges of the pumps, and the canopy above sagged, threatening to collapse under its own weight. It was as if time had forgotten this place, leaving it to decay in silence.

But what caught my eye was the charred remains of a car, its metal twisted and blackened. It looked like a skeletal frame, reduced to a hollow shell. The acrid smell of smoke still lingered in the air, a reminder of the violence that had taken place. I could see the outlines of two bodies inside, their forms distorted and grotesque, the heat of the fire leaving them in a state of near anonymity.

I felt bile rise in my throat as I approached the vehicle, the sight of the bodies sending a chill down my spine. They were unrecognizable, their features marred by the flames that had consumed them. It was a regular accident at first glance, but as I stepped closer, something caught my eye—a strange silhouette of a crow burned into the metal of the door. It was a grotesque symbol, almost mocking in its permanence, a stark reminder of the horror that had unfolded here.

The officers surrounding the scene moved with purpose, their voices low as they exchanged information. Some were taking photographs while others cordoned off the area with yellow tape, the bright color contrasting sharply with the soot and ash scattered across the ground. I could see their faces, grim and focused, but beneath that stoicism lay a shared disgust for the person responsible for this atrocity.

"Detective!" One of the officers called out, pulling me from my horrified reverie. It was Officer Harris, a veteran on the force whose grizzled demeanor spoke of years spent facing the darker sides of humanity. "We've got a preliminary ID on the victims. They're a couple, both in their thirties. They were reported missing a few days ago."

"Great," I muttered, my mind racing with the implications. A couple in their thirties, missing for days, now reduced to charred remains in a burnt-out car. "What about the crow?" I gestured toward the strange silhouette. "Any ideas on that?"

Harris frowned, his brow furrowing as he examined the burned metal. "No idea yet. It's too early to tell if it means something. Could be a sick joke, or it could be some kind of signature."

I nodded, feeling a sense of urgency wash over me. "We need to find out who did this. It's not just a homicide; it's a message."

The air felt heavy, thick with the scent of smoke and decay. I took a step back, forcing myself to breathe deeply, to regain my composure. The shock of the scene threatened to overwhelm me, but I couldn't let it. I had a job to do, and I wouldn't allow the horror to paralyze me.

I moved further away from the car, my gaze sweeping

over the gas station. There was something eerie about the way it stood, a testament to a past that had long since faded. The cracked pavement beneath my feet felt like a metaphor for the lives that had been shattered. Once a place of convenience, it was now a site of death, a macabre reminder of the darkness that lurked in the corners of the city.

"Get the forensics team out here," I called to another officer, my voice steady. "We need to gather every piece of evidence we can. And let's see if there are any surveillance cameras nearby."

The officers nodded, moving with renewed purpose. I could see them communicating with each other, their expressions a mix of determination and disgust. We all shared the same sentiment—anger at the person who had done this, a deep-seated rage that bubbled beneath the surface.

As I walked back toward the car, I caught sight of a few passersby who had gathered at a safe distance, their faces a mix of curiosity and horror. It was a reminder that this wasn't just a scene for us; it was a stark reality for the community. People often considered the police as detached, but in moments like this, the humanity of our work became painfully clear. We were here to protect, to serve, and to seek justice for those who could no longer speak for themselves.

"Detective, over here!" Officer Harris called out again, drawing my attention. He was crouched near the edge of the gas station, inspecting something on the ground. I approached, my heart pounding with anticipation.

"What did you find?" I asked, kneeling beside him.

He pointed to a series of footprints leading away from the scene, partially obscured by the debris. "Looks like someone was here right before the fire. We should get a cast of these."

I nodded, my mind racing with possibilities. "Let's get

that done. And check for any witnesses. Someone must have seen something."

The officers moved swiftly, and I felt a surge of adrenaline as I immersed myself in the investigation. The mix of emotions—anger, sadness, and determination—pushed me forward. I couldn't let the memory of those lost lives fade away; I needed to ensure they were given the justice they deserved.

As the forensic team arrived, I stepped aside to gather my thoughts. The scene was chaotic yet methodical, each officer focused on their task, working to piece together the puzzle that had led to this tragedy. I took a moment to breathe, inhaling the faint scent of gasoline mixed with the acrid smell of burnt rubber. It was a sensory overload, but I needed to stay sharp.

As I stood there, watching the professionals work, my mind drifted to the victims. I thought of their lives, their hopes, and dreams, now extinguished in such a violent manner. I felt a pang of sorrow for their families, the people who would never know what had happened to their loved ones. It was a reminder of why I had chosen this line of work —to fight for those who couldn't fight for themselves.

I approached Officer Harris again, who was speaking with one of the forensic specialists. "Any updates on the bodies?" I asked, my voice steady despite the turmoil inside me.

"Not yet," he replied, his expression grim. "They're still working on identifying them. But we'll have a preliminary report soon."

"Good," I said. "We need to find out who they are and what connections they might have had. This doesn't feel random."

He nodded, his eyes scanning the scene. "I agree. There's

something personal about this. The crow, the fire... it all feels deliberate."

I took a deep breath, steeling myself for what lay ahead. "Let's not lose sight of the bigger picture. We'll figure this out. We have to."

As the sun began to rise higher in the sky, casting its light over the gas station, I felt a renewed sense of determination. The shadows of the night were fading, but the memories of the victims would linger. We owed it to them to uncover the truth, to bring their killer to justice. I stood and watched as they removed what was left of the bodies and placed them on gurneys and put them in the ambulance. My fist clenched tightly. There was a monster here in Oklahoma and I planned on finding it.

CHAPTER 5

I headed back to headquarters, the weight of the morning's discovery pressing heavily on my shoulders. The symbol burned into the car's metal frame haunted my thoughts, its silhouette etched into my mind. I had seen that shape before, but where? It nagged at me like an itch I couldn't quite scratch, a puzzle piece that refused to fit.

As I entered the police station, the familiar sights and sounds enveloped me. The air was thick with the scent of stale coffee and the faint musk of worn upholstery. The walls were painted a dull beige, adorned with framed commendations and photographs of officers from years past. The hustle and bustle of the precinct felt like a living organism—detectives deep in conversation, officers typing away at keyboards, the occasional ring of a phone cutting through the ambiance.

I made my way to my desk, a cluttered testament to the chaos of my work. Papers were strewn about haphazardly, case files stacked precariously on one side, while coffee mugs half-filled with cold liquid sat like forgotten sentinels. A cork board loomed above my workspace, adorned with

MIKEL WILSON

photographs, notes, and string connecting different pieces of evidence. It was my organized chaos, a reflection of my thoughts, and right now, it felt like a battleground.

I grabbed my phone and dialed the forensic team, my heart racing with urgency. "I need a picture of the car now. There's something troubling me," I said, my voice steady despite the whirlwind of emotions churning inside me.

"On it, Detective," came the quick reply.

While I waited, I glanced around the station, noting the faces of my colleagues, their expressions a mix of determination and fatigue. I could see Officer Harris deep in conversation with another detective, his brow furrowed in concentration. The energy was palpable, a shared mission that united us all, but right now, my focus was singular. I needed that picture.

The phone buzzed, breaking my concentration. "I've sent the image to your email," the forensic technician informed me.

"Thank you," I replied, excitement coursing through me as I quickly opened my laptop. The screen flickered to life, and I navigated to my email, my pulse quickening as I downloaded the image.

As the photo popped up on the screen, I felt a rush of adrenaline. The charred remains of the car filled the frame, but it was the crow-shaped symbol that captured my attention. I stared at it, my mind racing as I tried to recall where I had seen something similar.

The dim light in my office flickered as I leaned closer, examining every detail of the burnt silhouette. The more I looked, the more familiar it became. I opened a new tab on my browser, typing in various keywords related to the symbol, but nothing came up. Frustration bubbled within me as I searched and searched, my thoughts swirling in a chaotic dance.

After what felt like hours, I decided to shift my approach. I pulled up our department's database and inserted the picture, hoping for a miracle. The computer hummed softly, processing my request, and I felt a knot tighten in my stomach. *What if I was grasping at straws? What if I was chasing a ghost?*

But then, the screen lit up with results. My heart raced as I scanned the findings. Similar burn marks, nearly identical to the one from the car, appeared on the screen. Each image told a story, each crow-shaped silhouette a chilling echo of the past. I leaned closer, squinting at the details, my breath catching in my throat as I processed the information.

"Over the last five years," I murmured to myself, "there have been several crows found outside burnt vehicles and buildings." The realization sent a shiver down my spine. What had once seemed like coincidences now felt like a thread connecting each horrifying event.

As I continued to scroll through the results, the implications of my findings crystallized in my mind. "We've got a serial killer on our hands," I whispered, the weight of the realization settling heavily in my chest. "He's been doing this under the radar for years."

Just then, Officer Harris stepped into my office, his brow furrowed with concern. "Hey, you okay? You've been at it for a while."

I turned to him, my heart racing with urgency as I shared my findings. "Harris, look at this!" I said, gesturing to the screen. "These burn marks—they're all linked to crows. There's a pattern here, and I think it's a serial killer."

Harris leaned closer, his eyes widening as he examined the images. "You're right. I've never seen anything like this. We need to bring this to the captain."

"Absolutely," I agreed, my mind racing with what we had to do next. "But first, let's gather more information. I want to see if there are any connections between the victims—any common threads that might lead us to the killer."

"Good call," he said, his voice steady. "I'll help you dig into the files."

We dove into the work, the hours blurring together as we sifted through case files. The room felt charged with energy as we pieced together the connections. With each name we uncovered, each detail we examined, the picture became clearer.

"Look at this," I said, pointing to a photograph of one of the previous victims. "She had a crow tattoo on her wrist. It's the same crow shape we've seen in the burn marks."

Harris's eyes widened as he nodded in understanding. "And the others had similar connections. It's almost like a calling card."

"Exactly," I said, feeling a surge of determination. "We need to reach out to their families. There has to be something more—some link between them that we haven't uncovered yet."

As the sun began to set outside, the sky transformed into a canvas painted with hues of orange, pink, and deep purple. The light filtered through the slatted blinds of my office, creating striped shadows that danced across the cluttered desk. Dust motes floated gracefully in the fading light, illuminated like tiny stars in a dimming sky. The air was thick with anticipation, heavy with the weight of the day's discoveries and the urgency of what lay ahead.

The room around me, once filled with the sterile scent of paper and old coffee, now felt charged with energy. Papers were strewn haphazardly across my desk—case files, photographs of victims, and hastily scribbled notes that chronicled my thoughts, each one a piece of the puzzle we were desperately trying to solve. A half-empty coffee mug, stained with reminders of long hours spent in this very spot, sat precariously close to the edge, a testament to my relentless pursuit of justice.

I could hear the distant hum of the precinct—phones ringing off the hook, voices of people murmuring, and the occasional clatter of boots on the tile floor. It formed a melodious rhythm. The familiar buzzing of noise helped me concentrate, and I felt the pieces fitting together in my mind, the connections forming like strands of an intricate web. The darkness of the situation loomed, threatening to engulf me, but I wouldn't give up until the monster was behind bars or dead. I inhaled deeply, allowing the familiar scents of my workspace to ground me—paper, ink, and the faint, lingering aroma of burnt coffee. I grabbed my notebook, its pages filled with scrawled thoughts and diagrams, and felt the coolness of its cover against my palm. "Let's get to work," I said, my voice steady, echoing with focus.

"We have a killer to catch."

With that, I plunged into the depths of my mission, ready to unravel the tangled threads of this grim tapestry. The setting sun cast a warm glow on my face, a fleeting reminder of the world outside, but in that moment, my focus was unwavering. Justice awaited, and I was determined to find it.

This weight ahead was daunting, but I was ready for the challenge. As I dove deeper into our research, Harris at some time had left. I looked up and he was gone but it didn't matter to me the atmosphere in the precinct shifted. The tension was palpable, but it was also charged with an unyielding need to succeed.

Every click of the keyboard, every whispered conversation, brought us closer to the truth. I could feel it in my bones—we were on the verge of uncovering something monumental. And as the night wore on, I knew that I wouldn't rest until I had brought the killer to justice. Now to tell the Captain my findings, this case has to be mine.

CHAPTER 6

I gathered my papers and photographs, carefully stacking them into a neat pile as I headed to Captain Howard's office. With each piece of evidence I touched, I felt a flicker of hope and determination. But that hope was tempered by the weight of uncertainty pressing down on me. The hallway was bustling with officers and detectives, their voices a low murmur punctuated by the occasional bark of laughter or the ringing of phones. Footsteps echoed against the linoleum floor, creating a rhythm that matched the frantic beating of my heart. Yet, my focus remained solely on what lay ahead—the captain's office.

As I walked, I couldn't shake the feeling of tension coiling within me. What would Captain Howard say? Would he understand the urgency of this case, the fire burning within me to find the truth? Each step felt heavier, as if I were dragging an anchor behind me. The discoveries I had made earlier that day weighed on my mind, and I knew I had to

FLAMES OF THE CROWS BETRAYAL

convince him to let me pursue this case. I couldn't let it slip away.

THE DOOR to his office was a solid oak, worn from years of use yet imposing in its stature. I paused for a moment, taking a deep breath to steady myself. I had faced difficult conversations before, but this felt different. There was so much at stake. I knocked lightly, the sound echoing in the quiet corridor. "Captain, it's me," I called out, my voice steady despite the anxiety swirling within me.

I TOOK A BREATH, gathering my thoughts. "Captain, I need to discuss the burned car homicide," I started, laying my papers on the desk in front of him. "I've uncovered some links that I believe are crucial to the case."

HIS GAZE PIERCED my body as he assessed me. "Aren't you currently being watched by Internal Affairs?"

MY STOMACH DROPPED at the mention of Internal Affairs. The scrutiny was suffocating, but I couldn't let it deter me. "Yes, but that doesn't change the fact that I'm the best person for this job," I argued, a fire igniting in my chest. "I can't let this slip through our fingers. There's a killer out there, and I need to pursue this lead."

THE CAPTAIN SAT behind his desk, a mountain of paperwork piled high in front of him. He looked up, his expression a mix of irritation and curiosity. "What do you want?"

MIKEL WILSON

. . .

"CAPTAIN, I need to talk to you about the homicide case—the one with the burned car," I said, laying my papers on the desk in front of him. "I've been doing some research, and I think I'm onto something."

I felt the heat of his scrutiny as I held his gaze, determination flooding my veins. I wouldn't back down. I couldn't.

CAPTAIN HOWARD LEANED back in his chair, crossing his arms over his chest. "You're under a microscope, Detective. I can't risk you getting too close to this case. It could blow back on the department, and I won't have that on my conscience."

FRUSTRATION BUBBLED WITHIN ME, but I kept my voice calm. "With all due respect, sir, I can handle this. I have a lead, and if I don't follow it, we could be missing out on a chance to catch a serial killer. The victims deserve justice."

HE SIGHED, rubbing the bridge of his nose as he considered my words. "I understand your passion, but I also need to protect the integrity of this investigation. If I let you pursue it, I'm going to assign you a partner."

THE KNOT in my stomach tightened. "A partner? Who?"

"SOMEONE I TRUST to keep an eye on you. I can't have you going rogue right now," he said, his voice firm but not unkind. "I'll allow you to work the case, but I need to ensure it's handled properly."

I OPENED my mouth to argue, but the weight of his authority stilled my words. "Fine," I relented, frustration simmering just below the surface. "I'll work with whoever you assign me."

"GOOD," he said, reaching for a file on his desk. "You'll meet your partner in a few minutes. Just remember, this is a team effort. Don't forget that."

BEFORE I COULD RESPOND, a knock echoed from the door, interrupting our conversation. "Come in," Captain Howard called out, his tone shifting to one of irritation.

THE DOOR SWUNG OPEN, and to my utter shock, Dom walked in with a bright smile on his face. The tension in the room melted away for a brief moment as I felt my heart leap in my chest. "Hey, what's going on?" he asked, glancing between the captain and me, his expression a mix of curiosity and concern.

"DETECTIVE," Captain Howard said, his voice taking on a more formal tone. "You're meeting your new partner."

DOM'S EYES widened slightly as he processed the information. "Wait, you're assigning me to work with her?"

"DON'T GET ANY IDEAS," Captain Howard warned, his gaze sharp. "This isn't a social call. You're here to keep things on the straight and narrow."

I SHOT a glare at the captain, feeling a mix of gratitude and frustration. "I'm perfectly capable of handling this case on my own," I said, my voice steady. "But if I have to work with someone, I'd prefer it to be Dom."

"GOOD," Dom replied, his smile widening as he stepped further into the office, the tension in the air dissipating slightly. "I can think of no one better to partner with."

CAPTAIN HOWARD RAISED AN EYEBROW, clearly not thrilled with the idea. "You two need to maintain professionalism. This is a serious case, and I expect you to treat it as such."

"OF COURSE, SIR," Dom said, his tone earnest. "We'll keep it professional. Right?" He turned to me, and I nodded, feeling a mix of relief and excitement at the prospect of working alongside him.

"EXCELLENT," Captain Howard said, his voice still carrying a weight of authority. "Now, get to work. There's a lot to do, and I expect regular updates on your progress."

As we stepped out of the captain's office, I felt a rush of exhilaration. "I can't believe he assigned us to work together," I said, my voice barely above a whisper as we walked down the hallway.

"Me neither," Dom replied, his eyes sparkling with enthusiasm. "But I'm glad. I think we'll make a great team."

"Yeah, but we need to be cautious," I said, my heart racing as I considered the implications. "With everything going on, I don't want Internal Affairs breathing down our necks."

"We'll keep our heads down," he reassured me, his expression serious yet kind. "Let's focus on the case and make sure we get justice for the victims."

I nodded, a sense of purpose igniting within me. "Right. We need to start by reviewing the evidence we have. There's so much to uncover."

The two of us made our way to the bustling heart of the precinct, the hum of activity swirling around us like a living organism. Officers moved with purpose, the sound of keyboards clacking filling the air as detectives exchanged information. The atmosphere was charged with a shared determination that resonated deeply within me.

. . .

MIKEL WILSON

As we reached my desk, I turned to see the chaos of papers and photographs spread out like a battlefield. "This is my organized chaos," I said with a small smile, gesturing at the mess. "Welcome to my world."

Dom chuckled, stepping closer to examine the notes I had made. "I see you've been busy. What do you have?"

"Take a look," I replied, pointing to the corkboard above my desk, where I had pinned photographs of the victims alongside newspaper clippings that hinted at the pattern I had uncovered. "This is what we're dealing with."

As he scanned the board, I could see the gears turning in his mind. "So, the crow symbol... that's what you think connects them?" he asked, his brow furrowing in concentration.

"Exactly," I said, leaning closer to him, the tension in my chest easing as we fell into the rhythm of collaboration. "I believe there's a deeper connection between these victims, and the crow has to mean something. We need to find out what."

Dom nodded, his expression shifting from curiosity to determination. "Let's start by identifying each victim's background. We should look into their relationships, their lives before they were taken. Maybe someone saw something."

. . .

FLAMES OF THE CROWS BETRAYAL

"GOOD IDEA," I agreed, feeling a spark of enthusiasm ignite between us. "We can split the work. I'll take the first victim's file, and you can start on the second."

"DEAL," he said, already pulling up the necessary documents on the computer.

AS WE DOVE into our work, the world around us faded away. The chaos of the precinct became a distant hum, and all that mattered was the task at hand. I could feel the weight of the investigation pressing down on me, but having Dom by my side made it feel more manageable.

WITH EACH PIECE of information we uncovered, the urgency of our mission became more pronounced. The sun dipped lower in the sky, casting long shadows across the room, but I felt a fire burning within me, fueled by the hope of justice.

"LET'S MAKE THIS COUNT," I said, glancing over at Dom, who was deep in concentration. "For the victims."

"FOR THE VICTIMS," he echoed, his gaze intense as he focused on the screen in front of him.

AS THE HOURS PASSED, we continued our investigation, pouring over files, connecting dots, and piecing together the puzzle that lay before us. With each piece of evidence, I felt the thrill of the chase—the adrenaline coursing through my veins, propelling us forward.

CHAPTER 7

After the shocking news that Dom was now my partner, the air between us felt thick with unspoken tension as we climbed into my car. The ride to the restaurant was marked by an awkward silence, punctuated only by the faint hum of the engine and the soft crackle of the radio, which I had left off. I could feel the weight of the moment pressing down on us, and I could sense Dom's uncertainty as he settled into the passenger seat.

I started the car and pulled away from the station, my mind racing with thoughts about the day's events. How had we gotten here? Just a few days ago, Dom had been a rookie, eager to learn the ropes, and now he was my partner, my boyfriend, and suddenly all of that seemed to carry a heavier weight. I stole a glance at him, his profile illuminated by the streetlights as we drove through the city. His brow was slightly furrowed, and I could see the tension in his jaw.

"Are you okay?" I asked, breaking the silence, my voice sounding more hesitant than I intended.

"Yeah, just... processing, I guess," he replied, his gaze fixed out the window. "This is a lot to take in."

I nodded, gripping the steering wheel a little tighter. "I know. I didn't expect it either. I thought you'd be paired with someone else, someone more experienced."

"Right? I mean, I didn't think they'd put me with my girl-friend, of all people," he said with a hint of a chuckle, but it fell flat, the laughter feeling more like a defense mechanism than genuine amusement.

"Guess they think we can handle it," I replied, forcing a smile. "Or maybe they just wanted to keep us on our toes."

"Or maybe they wanted to make sure you're following the rules," he said, his voice teasing, but I could sense the under-current of seriousness behind it.

"Stop," I said, glancing over at him, my heart racing again. "You're not here to watch me, are you?"

"Not unless you start breaking the law," he shot back, a playful smirk finally breaking through the tension. "Then I might have to arrest you."

"Ha ha, very funny," I said, but the humor didn't quite reach my eyes. I was still grappling with the idea that our relationship could be scrutinized in a way that could jeopar-dize everything we had built together.

The silence returned as we made our way through familiar streets, the city bustling with nightlife. I turned on the radio, hoping to fill the space with music, but the songs felt too loud, too intrusive. I fiddled with the dial, eventually settling on something soft and melodic, trying to ease the atmosphere.

"Do you have a place in mind?" Dom asked, breaking the silence again as we approached a busy intersection.

"Not really," I admitted. "I thought we could just find something on the way. What are you in the mood for?"

He shrugged, glancing at the passing restaurants. "I could go for something casual. Maybe a burger or pizza? Nothing too fancy tonight."

"Sounds good to me," I replied, scanning the area for options. "How about that new burger place on Elm? I've heard good things about it."

"Sure, I've been wanting to check that out," he said, visibly relaxing in his seat. "Plus, I've heard their fries are amazing."

"Fries can definitely help ease the stress," I said, a hint of humor creeping into my tone. The thought of crispy fries made my stomach growl in agreement, and I felt a little lighter as we headed toward Elm Street.

As we approached the restaurant, I noticed the neon sign glowing brightly against the backdrop of the dusky sky. The place was bustling, filled with the sounds of laughter and clinking glasses. My stomach fluttered with a mix of antici- pation and nerves. "Here we go," I said, parking the car and turning off the engine.

We stepped out into the cool evening air, and I could feel the energy of the city swirling around us. I glanced over at Dom, who seemed to take a deep breath, as if preparing himself for whatever conversation lay ahead. "Ready?" I asked, trying to muster some enthusiasm.

"Yeah, let's do this," he replied, his voice steady though his eyes betrayed a hint of uncertainty.

As we walked inside, we were greeted by the lively atmosphere of the restaurant. The smell of grilled meat and spices enveloped us, and the sound of sizzling burgers on the grill filled the air. We approached the host stand, and after a brief wait, he showed us to a cozy booth in the corner. I slid into the seat across from him, the tension between us still palpable, but I hoped that a good meal would work its magic.

"Do you want to start with some appetizers?" I asked, picking up the menu and flipping through it. "Maybe some loaded nachos?"

"Absolutely," he said, finally flashing a genuine smile. "I'm always down for nachos. And definitely fries. Can't forget those."

I chuckled, feeling the atmosphere lighten just a bit. "Okay, nachos and fries it is. And maybe a couple of burgers to share?"

"Sounds perfect," he replied, his eyes sparkling with enthusiasm. "I think I'll go for the classic cheeseburger. Can't go wrong with that."

"I might try the spicy jalapeño burger," I said, glancing at the menu again. "I need something to kick my taste buds into gear."

"Brave choice," he said, a hint of admiration in his tone. "You're going to regret that later when you're chugging water."

"Maybe," I admitted with a playful grin. "But life is too short for bland food, right?"

"True," he said, leaning back in his seat, clearly relaxing a little more. "You always know how to make the most of things."

As we placed our order with the server, I felt a sense of normalcy returning, the rhythm of our banter easing the tension that had lingered since we left the station. But as the food arrived and we dug into the appetizers, my mind still danced with thoughts of the day's events.

"Okay, let's talk about it," I said, breaking the comfortable silence that had settled over us as we shared the nachos.

"Talk about what?" Dom asked, his mouth full of food, a playful glint in his eyes.

"About us being partners," I said, my heart pounding as I prepared to open a conversation that felt necessary yet uncomfortable. "I mean, it's a big change for both of us."

"Yeah, it is," he replied, wiping his mouth with a napkin. "But I'm excited. I think we can make a great team. We already communicate well, and we know each other's strengths and weaknesses."

"True," I said, nodding slowly. "But it's also a lot of pressure. I don't want our personal relationship to affect our work dynamic. I need you to be able to speak up if you disagree with me."

"Of course," he said earnestly. "And I trust you to do the same. It's about being professional, right? We can separate the two, I promise."

"I hope so," I said, the knot in my stomach loosening just a bit as I looked into his eyes. "I just want to make sure we're on the same page."

"Me too," he replied, his voice steady. "And if anything feels off, we'll address it. But I'm not going to let anyone else's expectations dictate how we work together."

"Good," I said, feeling a flicker of relief. "Because I really value what we have, both in and out of the office."

He smiled, and in that moment, I felt the connection between us solidify, the tension of the day fading away. "Me too. I think we've got something special, and I'm looking forward to seeing how we can grow from this."

As we continued to eat, laughter and easy conversation flowed between us, the initial awkwardness of the ride to the restaurant dissipating like mist in the morning sun. We shared stories, joked about our day, and savored the food, feeling the warmth of companionship envelop us.

But in the back of my mind, the weight of the day still lingered. I knew the complexities of our situation wouldn't disappear overnight. Still, as I looked at Dom, a sense of hope began to blossom. Maybe, just maybe, we could navigate this together and emerge stronger on the other side.

The scent of garlic and fresh herbs wafted through the air, mingling with the faint aroma of grilled meats. I glanced across the table at Dom, who was scrolling through his phone, oblivious to the world around him. My heart swelled at the sight of him—his brows furrowed in concentration. He was undeniably handsome, and I couldn't help but smile, even as unease lingered just beneath the surface.

"Dom," I said, breaking the comfortable silence. "Are you ready to dig into this case? We've got a lot to cover."

"Yeah, I'm on it," he replied, finally looking up. The hint of a smile tugged at his lips, and I felt myself relax a little. "I've been going over the files all day. There are some leads I think we should follow up on."

"Good," I said, leaning forward, eager to hear his thoughts. "What have you got?"

CHAPTER 8

NATALIE

*A*s he began to explain his ideas, I found myself torn between admiration and anxiety. Dom had a natural instinct for this line of work, and I was grateful to have him as my partner. But the very fact that we were partners—him being my boyfriend and me his superior—made the dynamics complicated. Would he see me as a partner in a professional sense, or would he always feel the weight of my authority?

And then there was the nagging thought that perhaps the captain had orchestrated this pairing for a reason. What if he was watching me? What if the captain had doubts about my ability to lead and had assigned Dom to keep tabs on me?

"Are you listening?" Dom's voice broke through my spiraling thoughts. I blinked and focused on him, forcing a smile.

"Of course. Sorry, I was just…thinking."

MIKEL WILSON

He raised an eyebrow, a teasing smirk dancing on his lips. "Thinking about me, huh?"

"Something like that," I replied, trying to keep my tone light. "So tell me more about those leads."

As he dove back into the case, detailing the inconsistencies he had found in witness statements, I felt a mix of pride and confusion. There was something so genuine about his passion for the job, and it reminded me of why I was drawn to him in the first place. But the more I engaged with him professionally, the more I wondered if our relationship would be scrutinized.

"Do you think we should follow up with the bartender from that night?" he asked, his brows furrowing as he considered the implications of what we had learned so far.

"Definitely," I said, nodding. "If he saw anything suspicious, it could lead us to the suspect."

"Let's set that up for tomorrow," he suggested, his eyes lighting up with enthusiasm.

"Sounds like a plan," I replied, my heart warming. He had an infectious energy that made even the toughest cases feel manageable. But as I watched him, I couldn't shake the feeling that there was more at play here.

"Hey," I said, my voice softer now. "Can I ask you something?"

"Sure," he said, leaning back in his seat, a hint of curiosity tugging at his features.

I hesitated, unsure of how to frame my thoughts. "Do you ever think about why they put us together as partners? I mean, it seems a little too perfect, doesn't it? You, a rookie, paired up with the sergeant?"

He chuckled softly, but his expression shifted to one of contemplation. "I think it was a good move. You're a great leader, and I can learn a lot from you. Plus, we already know how to communicate well."

"Right," I said, forcing a smile. "But don't you think it's a bit odd? I mean, you're still figuring out the ropes, and here I am, your superior. What if they're watching me? What if they think I'm not doing my job right?"

Dom's brows knitted together as he processed my words. "Are you serious? You really think the captain would assign me to keep an eye on you? That's ridiculous."

"Is it?" I countered, my heart racing at the thought. "I mean, you're still new, and I'm the one who's been here longer. Maybe they think I need a babysitter."

"Come on, that's not fair," he said, leaning forward. "You're one of the best in the department. You've proven yourself time and again. I'm just here to learn from you, not to watch your back."

"Then why do I feel like you're being put in a position to monitor me?" I shot back, unable to mask the frustration in my voice.

Dom's expression softened, and he reached across the table, taking my hand in his. "You know I'd never do that to you, right? I'm here because I want to be, not because someone told me to keep tabs on you. You mean too much to me for that."

I looked down at our hands, the warmth of his touch grounding me. "I know, but the thought is still there. I can't help but wonder…"

"Wonder what?" he prompted gently, his thumb brushing against my knuckles.

"What if you're a mole?" I blurted out, the words spilling from my lips before I could stop myself. "What if the captain sent you to make sure I'm following the rules? If you are, I swear to God I will kill you, Dom."

He laughed, a deep, genuine sound that cut through the tension in the air. "You've got to be kidding me! Me? A mole? That's a little dramatic, don't you think?"

"Maybe," I said, my heart still racing. "But it's a possibility. You know how the department works. The politics of it all can be brutal."

"Listen," he said, his voice steady. "I promise you, I'm not here to report back to the captain. I'm here to learn from you, and I'm excited about it. I wouldn't want it any other way."

I met his gaze, searching for any hint of deception, but all I found was sincerity. "Okay, but what if you're being used as a pawn? What if they think you need to keep me in check?"

"Then I'll just have to prove them wrong," he said, squeezing my hand. "I trust you, and I trust your judgment. If anyone has the right to be in this position, it's you."

His words wrapped around me like a comforting blanket, but doubts still lingered at the edges of my mind. "You know the captain can be unpredictable. He has a way of making you feel like you're under a microscope."

"Yeah, but that's just part of the job, isn't it?" Dom replied, his tone lightening. "You're not the only one under scrutiny. I've got my own challenges to face. If anything, we can help each other navigate it."

I released a breath I didn't realize I was holding, feeling a sense of relief wash over me. "You're right. I just wish I didn't have to feel this way."

"Look, if it helps, I'm just as nervous about this partnership as you are," he admitted, a hint of vulnerability creeping into his voice. "I don't want to disappoint you or anyone else in the department. I want to prove myself."

"You're doing great," I said, trying to reassure him. "You've got the skills, and you've got the passion. Just remember that I'm here for you, too. We're in this together."

"Together," he echoed, his eyes sparkling with warmth. "And if the captain thinks I'm here to keep tabs on you, then he's in for a surprise."

I chuckled, finally feeling some of the tension ease. "We'll show him what we're made of, won't we?"

"Absolutely," he replied, his smile infectious. "But right now, let's focus on the case. What's next on our list?"

As we shifted back into work mode, I couldn't shake the feeling that our partnership was more than just a professional arrangement. There was a bond between us that transcended the confines of the job, a connection that made everything feel more significant. Yet, the shadow of uncertainty still loomed over me.

Could I truly trust him? Would he remain loyal, or would he be swayed by the pressures of the department?

I pushed those thoughts aside and concentrated on the present, determined to make the most of our time together. As the conversation flowed, punctuated by laughter and shared ideas, I felt the anxiety begin to lift.

After our satisfying dinner, the cozy hum of the restaurant began to fade, but Dom's gaze brightened as he leaned back in his seat, a hint of mischief dancing in his eyes. "You know what would make this night even better?" he asked, his voice low and teasing.

"What's that?" I replied, arching an eyebrow, already anticipating what he might say.

"Chocolate cake," he declared, his enthusiasm infectious. "We can't leave this place without a slice."

I chuckled, shaking my head. "Dom, we really don't need dessert. We practically inhaled those nachos and fries."

"Come on, it's a special occasion!" he insisted, a playful pout forming on his lips. "We should celebrate our new partnership. Besides, it's chocolate cake. How can you say no to that?"

I hesitated, weighing the desire for something sweet against the lingering thoughts of the day. But as I looked into his hopeful eyes, I felt my resolve start to crumble. "Fine," I relented with a laugh. "But just one slice to share."

"Perfect!" he exclaimed, waving down the server to place our order.

A few moments later, the server returned with a generous slice of rich chocolate cake, its layers stacked high and drizzled with glossy ganache. The sight of it made my mouth water, and I felt a rush of excitement as I took in the dessert before us. It was decadent, the kind of cake that demanded to be savored.

Dom slid a fork over to me, a playful glint in his eye. "Ladies first," he said, grinning.

I couldn't help but smile back. "So chivalrous," I teased, picking up the fork and taking a bite. The chocolate melted on my tongue, rich and velvety, and I closed my eyes in delight. "Oh wow, this is amazing."

"Right?" he said, taking a bite himself. "I told you it was worth it."

We took turns feeding each other bites, the playful exchanges filled with laughter and lighthearted banter. Each forkful was shared with smiles and whispers, our fingers brushing against each other as we savored the sweet moment together. It felt like a small celebration of us amidst the chaos of the day.

As we finished the last bites, I felt a sense of warmth and contentment settle over me. The anxiety that had lingered since we left the station seemed to melt away, replaced by something lighter, something that made my heart swell. "I'm glad we did this," I said, looking into his eyes.

"Me too," Dom replied, his expression softening. "It's nice to take a moment and just enjoy each other's company."

We paid the bill, and as we walked back to the car, I felt a weight lift off my shoulders. The night air was cool, and the sounds of the city wrapped around us, a comforting backdrop to our quiet conversation. Dom's presence felt grounding, and I found myself leaning closer to him as we walked, relishing the warmth radiating from his side.

Once we reached the car, he opened the door for me, and I slid into the seat, a smile spreading across my face. As he got in and shut the door, he reached over and took my hand, intertwining our fingers tightly. The simple gesture sent a warm rush through me, and I couldn't help but squeeze his hand back.

The drive back to our apartment was filled with a peaceful silence, the kind that spoke volumes without the need for words. I stole glances at him as he focused on the road, his features illuminated by the dashboard lights. There was an ease in the air, a familiarity that made my heart flutter. I couldn't remember the last time I felt so connected to him, so at peace.

As we pulled into the parking lot, Dom kept holding my hand, his grip reassuring and warm. "You okay?" he asked softly, his eyes flicking toward me for a moment before returning to the road.

"Yeah, I'm good," I replied, the honesty in my voice surprising me. "I feel... lighter, I guess."

"Good," he said, a smile breaking across his face. "That's how it should be. We can tackle anything together."

Once we parked, we stepped out of the car and made our way to the apartment. The night sky stretched above us, stars twinkling like little diamonds against the dark canvas of the universe. I felt a sense of gratitude wash over me—a realization that despite the challenges we faced, we had each other.

Inside the apartment, the familiar warmth enveloped me, and I took a moment to breathe it all in. "I'm going to take a shower to wash away the stress of the day," I said, turning to Dom. "Want to join?"

He chuckled, and I could see the playful glint in his eye.

"As tempting as that sounds, I think I'll pass this time. I'd probably end up stealing all the hot water."

"Fair point," I laughed, shaking my head. "But you're missing out."

"Next time," he promised, a genuine smile tugging at his lips. "I'll save the hot water for you."

With a final squeeze of my hand, I headed to the bathroom, the sound of running water filling the silence as I stepped under the warm stream. The heat enveloped me, and I closed my eyes, letting the water wash away the stress and worries of the day. I felt the tension in my shoulders slowly dissipate, and I couldn't help but think of how lucky I was to have Dom in my life.

After a few minutes, I emerged from the shower, wrapped in a soft towel, my hair damp and tousled. The bathroom was filled with steam, and I inhaled deeply, feeling refreshed. I stepped into the living room, and Dom was sitting on the couch, looking relaxed as he scrolled through his phone.

"Hey, you look fantastic," he said, glancing up and giving me an appreciative smile.

"Thanks," I replied, feeling a blush creep up my cheeks. "I feel a lot better."

He patted the space beside him, and I wandered over, settling in close to him. The warmth of his body next to mine felt comforting, and I instinctively leaned into him, resting my head on his shoulder. He slipped an arm around me, pulling me closer, and I reveled in the tenderness of the moment.

"I've been thinking," he said softly, breaking the comfortable silence. "About how we can make this partnership work, both at work and at home."

"Me too," I admitted, tilting my head to look up at him. "It's going to be a bit of a balancing act, but I really believe we can do it."

"Absolutely," he replied, his voice steady and reassuring. "We just need to keep communicating and be honest with each other. We can't let anything come between us."

"Agreed," I said, feeling a spark of excitement at the thought of our journey together. "We've faced challenges before, and we've always come out stronger."

He smiled, his eyes shining with affection. "And I wouldn't want to go through it with anyone else but you."

In that moment, I felt a rush of love and gratitude. I leaned in closer, pressing a soft kiss to his cheek, then pulled back to meet his gaze. "Thank you for being you, Dom. You make everything feel more manageable."

He leaned in, brushing his lips against mine in a tender kiss that sent butterflies flitting through my stomach. "And thank you for being my anchor. I'll always be here for you."

As we settled into the comfortable rhythm of each other's presence, I felt a sense of hope and warmth envelop us. The worries of the day faded into the background, leaving only the sweetness of our connection. I knew we had a long road ahead, but as I nestled against him, I felt ready to face whatever challenges came our way, hand in hand.

CHAPTER 9

DOM

The training gym was an echoing cavern of sweat and determination, with walls adorned in black and red that absorbed the fervor of countless fighters before us. The air was thick with the mingling scents of chalk, worn-out shoes, and the faint tang of metal from the wrestling mats that sprawled across the floor. Sunlight filtered through high windows, casting harsh beams that illuminated the dust swirling in the air, a reminder of the countless hours spent here, honing skills for an unforgiving world.

The mats themselves were a patchwork of vibrant colors, their surface slightly springy yet firm, designed to cushion falls but also to provide a solid ground for grappling. They absorbed the noise of our movements—the thud of bodies hitting the ground, the scuffing of feet, and the breaths that came in sharp gasps. The mats were well-worn, the edges fraying, but they held stories of resilience and the struggle against one's limits.

Natalie squared off against me, her posture tense, a coiled spring ready to explode. Her red hair was pulled back into a tight ponytail, accentuating the determination etched across her brow. The training gear she wore—a fitted rash guard and grappling shorts—clung to her athletic frame, emphasizing the strength that lay beneath the surface. This wasn't just a workout for her; it was a battleground where she could fight her demons, and I knew it.

"Alright, let's start easy," I said, raising my hands in a pacifying gesture, hoping to ease her into the session. But there was a fire in her eyes, a flickering rage that hinted at a deeper turmoil. "Just focus on technique."

"Technique?" she scoffed, her voice laced with sarcasm. "You think I'm going to just stand here and let you throw me around? Not a chance."

Before I could respond, she lunged at me with an intensity that caught me off guard. I barely had time to react as she closed the distance between us, her body weight crashing into mine like a wave. We tumbled onto the mat, her momentum carrying us both into a roll. She was strong, and I had to remind myself that this was training, not a fight for survival.

"Whoa, Natalie!" I grunted, trying to shift my weight and regain control. "Calm down! We're supposed to be training together!"

But she was relentless, her focus narrowing to a single point. She pushed me as I tried to maneuver into a better position, attempting to secure a dominant hold. Her arms wrapped around mine, and I felt her muscles tense, a vise grip that spoke of her refusal to back down. I knew that under normal circumstances, she had the potential to be a formidable opponent, but today, something was eating away at her.

"Come on, show me what you've got!" she shouted, her voice rising. "I'm not going to hold back!"

With a swift move, she transitioned into a mount, her knees pressing into my ribs, pinning me down. "You think this is a game? You think I'm just going to let you take me down without a fight?"

"Just… just breathe," I gasped, trying to squirm out from beneath her. "I'm not your enemy! Let's work on this!"

But that only fueled her fire. She pressed her weight down harder, a fierce determination radiating from her as if she were wrestling with unseen demons, battling against something far more intense than our sparring session. I could see it in the way her jaw clenched, the way her breath came in sharp, uneven bursts. She was fighting against herself, and I was merely the vessel for her frustrations.

"You don't understand!" she yelled, her voice cracking with emotion. "I can't afford to lose! Not again!"

I managed to roll her off of me, grabbing her wrist and spinning into a dominant position. "Natalie, listen to me! It's okay to let your guard down sometimes! You need to trust me!"

But her eyes were wild, flickering with a mix of anger and fear. She broke free from my hold with a sudden burst of energy, transitioning into a standing position, her fists clenched at her sides. "Trust? Trust is what got Marcus killed! You think I'm going to let my guard down? Not a chance!"

Her words struck me like a physical blow, the raw pain and terror behind them evident. Marcus—a name that hung in the air between us like a specter, a reminder of the stakes we faced. It was a name that echoed in the hallways of our memories of her partner that died in her arms, a constant reminder of what could happen if we weren't prepared, if we let our defenses falter.

"Marcus wouldn't want you to do this to yourself!" I shouted back, my frustration boiling over. "He would want you to fight smart, not just hard! You're not honoring his memory by being reckless!"

The challenge hung in the air, a palpable tension that enveloped us. For a moment, we stood there, both of us breathing heavily, the world around us fading away, leaving only the two of us and our unresolved emotions. I could see the conflict in her eyes—the desire to push through, to prove herself, clashing with the sorrow that threatened to drown her.

"Prove myself?" she echoed, her voice softer now, almost a whisper. "What does that even mean anymore? I can't just forget…"

At that moment, I stepped forward, closing the distance between us, my hands reaching out to grasp her shoulders firmly. "You don't have to forget, Natalie. But you can't let fear control you. You have to learn to channel it, to use it to make you stronger, not to tear you apart."

She looked down, her breath hitching as she fought against the tide of emotions threatening to overwhelm her. I could see the struggle etched into her features, the fight between her instincts and the truth that echoed in my words.

"Let's take a step back," I said gently, relaxing my grip. "We'll slow it down. I promise, it's okay to be vulnerable. It's okay to feel scared. You're not alone in this."

She lifted her gaze, and for a brief moment, the fire in her eyes flickered, replaced by uncertainty. "But what if I lose control again? What if I hurt you?"

"You won't," I assured her, my voice steady. "We're training. We're here to learn, to grow. I trust you, and you need to trust yourself."

Natalie took a deep breath, the tension in her shoulders softening just slightly. "I don't know if I can."

The gym was a battleground of emotions, and tonight, it felt more like a cage than a training space. The air was heavy, thick with the scent of sweat and fear, a palpable tension that clung to the walls like a shroud. I had always known that our training sessions were about more than just fighting; they were about confronting our demons. But tonight, as Natalie stood before me, I felt the weight of her darkness pressing down on both of us.

"Of course you can," I assured her, my voice steady despite the turmoil inside me, as she kicked me hard in the gut. The impact jolted through my body, and the air rushed out of my lungs in a painful whoosh. I doubled over, gasping for breath, but even in that moment, I could see the fire in her eyes—a fierce determination mixed with a desperation that tore at my heart.

"Weakness will only get you killed," she hissed, a sharp edge to her voice that cut deeper than any physical blow. Her words echoed in the cavernous gym, a chilling reminder of the stakes we faced, and I struggled to push through the pain.

I knelt on the mat, fighting to regain my breath, my vision blurring for a moment as I looked up at her. She stood there, a warrior caught in the throes of her own internal battle, her fists clenched at her sides, trembling with pent-up energy. I could see the conflict raging within her, a tempest of grief and rage that threatened to consume her whole.

"Nat, listen to me," I said, my voice hoarse as I reached out for her. "You're not weak. You're fighting for something bigger than yourself. We're in this together."

But she turned away, her back rigid as she threw me a towel. "Clean up. Let's go home," she said, her voice flat and devoid of the warmth I had come to know. The dismissal stung, but I understood it was her way of coping, a method to shield herself from the pain that was clawing at her heart.

The ride home was tense, the silence between us thick

with unspoken words. I gripped the steering wheel tighter, my knuckles whitening as I searched for the right things to say. I wanted to reach her, to pull her out of the darkness that clouded her thoughts, but every time I opened my mouth, the words felt inadequate, like they would only push her further away.

As the city blurred past us, I stole glances at her from the corner of my eye. She stared out the window, her expression inscrutable, but I could sense the storm brewing beneath the surface. The weight of Marcus's death was a palpable force between us, and I knew that she was carrying it like a heavy shroud, suffocating her spirit.

CHAPTER 10

DOM

"Natalie," I finally said, my voice breaking the suffocating silence. "We need to talk about what happened today. You're not alone in this. I'm here for you."

Her head snapped in my direction, her eyes blazing with a mix of anger and pain. "What's there to talk about?" she shot back, her tone sharp. "Marcus is dead, and we're still out there searching for a killer who's slipping through our fingers! I can't afford to feel sorry for myself!"

I clenched my jaw, frustrated by her refusal to acknowledge the depth of her grief. "But you're hurting, Nat! You can't just bury it beneath anger and determination. That's not going to bring him back!"

"Don't you dare say that!" she screamed, her voice echoing in the confined space of the car. "You don't understand! I should have been there for him. I could have saved him! If I don't catch this guy, then what's the point? What's the point of any of it?"

Her words hit me like a punch to the gut, a painful reminder of the burden she felt she had to carry. I could see it in her eyes, the guilt and the sense of responsibility that weighed her down, like an anchor pulling her into an abyss. "You're not responsible for what happened to him," I insisted, my voice softer now, trying to break through the walls she had built around herself. "You can't shoulder that alone. It's not your fault."

Natalie shook her head vehemently, her fists clenched so tightly that her knuckles turned white. "If I had been there, if I had been stronger... he might still be alive! I can't let that happen again. I can't let another victim slip away!"

Her passion ignited a fire within me, but I knew that it was fueled by pain and regret. "But if you keep pushing yourself like this, you're going to burn out. You need to grieve, to let it out. It's okay to feel weak sometimes. It doesn't make you any less of a fighter."

She turned to me, her eyes shimmering with unshed tears, and for a brief moment, I saw the vulnerability beneath her tough exterior. "I can't... I can't afford to be weak. Not now. Not after what happened to Marcus."

I reached over, placing my hand on her knee, hoping to convey the warmth and support that my words struggled to express. "It's okay to let your guard down with me. You don't have to be strong all the time. I'm here to help you carry that weight."

Her gaze dropped to my hand, and I could see the war raging inside her. "You don't understand," she said quietly, her voice trembling. "It's not just about me. It's about all the people out there who are still in danger. I can't let the fear take over. I can't let it paralyze me."

"No, but you can't let it consume you either," I replied gently. "You have to find a balance. You can fight for justice and still allow yourself to heal. It's not a weakness to care about yourself."

She turned to look out the window again, the tears finally spilling over as she blinked rapidly. "I just keep thinking about him. About how he was so full of life, and now... he's gone. And I was supposed to protect him. I was supposed to be there."

"It's okay to mourn him, Nat. It's okay to miss him," I urged, my heart aching for her. "Marcus wouldn't want you to torture yourself like this. He'd want you to keep fighting, yes, but not at the expense of your own life."

The quiet that followed was heavy, filled with the weight of our shared grief. I watched as she wrestled with her emotions, the storm inside her slowly beginning to quiet. She took a deep breath, her shoulders sagging slightly as the tension began to ease.

"I just... I don't know how to stop feeling this way," she admitted, her voice barely above a whisper. "I don't know how to let go."

"Maybe you don't have to let go completely," I suggested softly. "But you can learn to carry it differently. You can turn that pain into fuel, into strength, but you have to allow yourself to feel it first. You can't outrun your emotions forever."

"I'm not running!" Natalie snapped, her voice sharp enough to cut through the tension that filled the car. Her arms folded tightly across her chest, a physical barrier that seemed to shut me out completely. I could feel the weight of her anger and grief pressing down on me, a suffocating cloud that I couldn't disperse.

The ride home was a heavy silence, punctuated only by the hum of the engine and the rush of the wind through the cracks of the window. I stole glances at her, hoping to catch a glimpse of the woman I knew beneath the anger, but she was a fortress, her walls fortified against my attempts to reach her. When we finally pulled into the parking lot of our apartment, she exited the car without a word, leaving me alone with my thoughts, the disappointment gnawing at my insides.

A fine mess you've got yourself into, Dom. a bitter reminder that despite my best efforts, I had failed to connect with her when she needed me most. *Note to self: you will never understand women.*

The sound of the shower echoed through our apartment as I trudged inside, the familiar rhythm of water hitting tile a stark contrast to the chaos in my mind. I wanted to be there for her, to comfort her in whatever way I could. I wanted to step into that shower with her, to hold her close and remind her that she wasn't alone. But when I turned the knob of the bathroom door, my heart sank. It was locked.

I stood there for a moment, hand resting on the doorknob as the water cascaded down, a relentless torrent that reminded me of the tears I knew she was holding back. I wanted to break down the door, to tell her that I was here, that I would never leave her side, but I also knew that pushing wouldn't help. So I waited, listening to the sound of water echoing in the small space, wishing desperately that I could be the one to wash away her pain.

After what felt like an eternity, she finally emerged from the bathroom, steam billowing out behind her like a ghost escaping from its prison. Her face was devoid of expression, her eyes red-rimmed but dry. She walked past me without a word, and I felt the ache of her silence deep in my chest. I chose not to fight it; I had learned that sometimes, silence was all she needed.

I wandered into the bathroom after she left, the air thick with humidity and the faint scent of her soap. I turned the shower back on, letting the hot water cascade over my skin, hoping it would ease the pain in my heart. I pressed my forehead against the cool tiles, letting the water wash over me, drowning out the noise in my head.

What could I say? What did she need to hear? I felt utterly lost, a ship adrift in a stormy sea of emotions. I could feel the weight of Marcus's death hanging over us like a dark cloud, and I wished I had the words to lift it, to bring some light back into her eyes. But instead, I was left standing in the shower, water pouring over me, trying to wash away my own helplessness.

When I finally stepped out, I felt a little lighter, but the burden of my unspoken words still clung to me. I found a blanket and a pillow on the couch, an indication that she had retreated into her own world, and I knew then that I would be sleeping alone tonight. I wrapped myself in the blanket, the fabric soft against my skin, but it did little to soothe the ache in my heart.

*Maybe she just needs her space,*deep down, I knew it wasn't just space she needed; it was healing, and I was desperate to be a part of that process.

I lay on the couch, the familiar contours of the fabric feeling foreign beneath me. The living room was dim, the glow of the streetlights outside casting shadows across the walls. I stared at the ceiling, my mind racing with thoughts of Natalie, of Marcus, of everything that had happened. I tossed and turned, trying to find a comfortable position, but no matter how I shifted, sleep eluded me.

Why couldn't I find the right words? Why couldn't I reach her? The questions spiraled in my mind, each one more insistent than the last. I kept replaying the day's events, the look on her face when she kicked me, the anger in her voice, and the impenetrable wall she had built around herself. *How could I help her?*

Hours passed, the clock ticking away in the background as I lay there, restless and frustrated. The couch felt too small, too confining, as if it were trapping me in my own thoughts. I could hear the faint sound of her moving around in the apartment, but I didn't dare get up to check on her. I didn't want to intrude; I didn't want to push her further away.

Finally, as fatigue weighed down my eyelids, I slipped into a fitful sleep, my dreams filled with images of Natalie's face—angry, sad, lost. Each time I reached out for her, she slipped through my fingers like smoke, and I woke with a start, heart racing, drowning in a sense of helplessness.

I could still hear the water running in my mind, the echo of our earlier confrontation haunting me. I wanted to scream, to shake her and tell her that it was okay to feel, that it was okay to let her guard down. But every time I imagined saying those words, I felt a sense of futility wash over me.

As the night wore on, the living room felt colder, the shadows creeping in as if they were trying to claim me. I wrapped the blanket tighter around my shoulders, but it didn't keep out the chill of isolation, the ache of being so close yet so far from the woman I cared about. I could hear her moving around, but every time I thought about getting up, a wave of uncertainty stopped me.

What if she didn't want to talk? What if my presence only made things worse? I felt trapped in a cage of my own making, torn between the desire to comfort her and the fear of pushing her away even further.

In the depths of my restless thoughts, I realized that I couldn't keep this up. I needed to find a way to reach her, to let her know that she didn't have to face this darkness alone. But as I lay there, the shadows lengthening in the corners of the room, I felt utterly lost, and for the first time, I wondered if I was strong enough to carry both our burdens.

MIKEL WILSON

With a heavy heart, I closed my eyes and surrendered to the darkness. If there was a chance to save her I would do whatever it would take even if it killed me.

CHAPTER 11

NATALIE

The morning light filtered through the blinds, casting striped shadows across the bedroom floor. It felt like a spotlight on my guilt, illuminating the chaos within me. I lay in bed, staring at the ceiling, the weight of my thoughts pressing down on my chest. Why had I treated Dom like that? The anger, the grief, the overwhelming desire for justice—it was all spiraling out of control, and in my fury, I had pushed away the one person who loved me most.

I rolled over, the sheets twisted around me like a cocoon, but instead of bringing comfort, they felt suffocating. Memories of Marcus flooded my mind—his laughter, his warmth, the way he always had a joke to lighten the mood. Now, all that remained were shadows and echoes of what had been, and the pain of loss was a constant reminder that I was still fighting a war I couldn't seem to win.

I reached for my phone, my fingers trembling as I dialed Alicia's number. It felt like a lifeline, a connection to

MIKEL WILSON

someone who could help me navigate the storm inside my head. "Hello, this is Natalie. Do you have any openings?"

Alicia's voice was calm and steady, a soothing balm to my frayed nerves. "Of course, Natalie. Come in immediately. We can talk."

"Thank you," I whispered, barely able to contain the wave of emotion bubbling up inside me. I hung up, quickly dressing in a pair of jeans and a comfortable sweater, hoping that perhaps I could catch Dom before he left for the day. I needed to apologize, to show him that I regretted my behavior, that I didn't want to lose him.

But when I stepped into the living room, my heart sank. The couch was neatly arranged, the blanket folded, a pillow resting on the armrest—a clear sign that he had already left. I felt as if the air had been sucked out of the room, leaving me gasping. I had lost my chance to make things right.

Frustration and regret coursed through me as I got into my car, the engine purring to life. I turned on the radio, letting the soft, sappy music wash over me as I drove to Alicia's office. The melodies wrapped around my heart, amplifying the ache I felt inside. I could feel the tears welling in my eyes, blurring my vision as I navigated the familiar streets.

When I arrived, I took a deep breath, trying to compose myself before stepping into the office. The waiting room was filled with the scent of lavender and chamomile, a calming aroma that usually put me at ease. But today, it felt like an unforgiving reminder of my turmoil. Holding back the tears that threatened to spill over, I gingerly took my seat in front of Alicia.

"What's going on, Natalie?" she asked, her voice warm and inviting, a gentle prompt that was all I needed to unleash the torrent of emotions I had been holding back.

As soon as the words left her lips, the dam broke. "Everything is falling apart, Alicia!" I exclaimed, my voice cracking with the weight of my sorrow. "I pushed Dom away, and I don't know how to fix it! All this anger from losing Marcus... it's consuming me, and I'm taking it out on the people I love!"

Alicia watched me with a patient expression, her eyes filled with understanding. "Take a deep breath, Natalie. Let's unpack this together."

I nodded, trying to steady my racing heart. "I was so focused on finding the killer, on avenging Marcus, that I forgot about everything else. I didn't even think about how Dom was feeling. I treated him like he was the enemy, and now... I feel so alone."

"A lot of people handle grief in different ways," she said softly, leaning forward slightly. "You're carrying a heavy burden, and it's understandable that you might lash out. But it's important to acknowledge that it's not just about finding the killer; it's about healing yourself as well."

"I know that!" I snapped, the frustration bubbling up again. "But I don't know how to heal! I keep replaying that night in my head, and I can't escape it. I feel like I'm drowning, and I don't want to drag Dom down with me."

Alicia nodded, her demeanor calm and steady. "It's important to remember that you don't have to go through this alone. Dom cares about you, Natalie. He wants to be there for you, but you have to let him in. You can't push him away because you're afraid of what he might see."

I buried my face in my hands, the tears spilling over as I let out a sob. "I didn't mean to hurt him. I just... I was so angry. I wanted to be strong, to have control over something when everything felt so chaotic. But I took it out on him, and now he's gone."

"Have you considered talking to him? Apologizing for how you treated him?" Alicia asked, her voice gentle but firm.

MIKEL WILSON

"Yes, but what if he doesn't forgive me?" I whispered, my heart clenching at the thought. "What if I've pushed him too far?"

"Forgiveness is a process, Natalie. It takes time, and it often requires vulnerability. You have to be willing to show Dom your true self, the parts that are scared and hurt. It's okay to be vulnerable. It doesn't make you weak; it makes you human."

I took a shaky breath, her words resonating deep within me. "But what if he sees me as broken? What if he realizes that I'm not the person he thought I was?"

"You are still you, Natalie. Grief changes us, but it doesn't erase who we are. You have to let him see that you're struggling and that you need his support. It's okay to ask for help."

I nodded, but the knot in my stomach tightened even further. Alicia's words echoed in my mind, but the weight of my emotions felt unbearable. I took a deep breath, trying to steady myself, but the moment was shattered when my phone rang, the shrill sound piercing through the fragile cocoon of vulnerability I was wrapped in.

"Another body has been found," I said, my voice barely above a whisper as I glanced at the screen. The urgency of the situation gripped me, pulling me back into a world where my pain felt trivial compared to the horrors unfolding out there. "I have to go."

"Natalie," Alicia said, her tone firm as she stood up from her desk, her expression a mixture of concern and frustration. "You can't keep running from your emotions. You need to deal with what you're feeling, or it will consume you."

"I will deal with them when I have time!" I snapped, the words spilling out before I could stop myself. The fire in my voice surprised me, a sudden surge of defiance against the very feelings I had been struggling to confront. I felt like I was back in control, even if just for a moment. "I have to go."

Without waiting for her response, I rushed out the door and into my car, the engine rumbling to life as I slammed the door shut. The familiar weight of the badge on my hip felt like a lifeline, grounding me amid the chaos. But as I drove, my thoughts began to spiral again, the tension mounting. What poor soul had been tortured by the Crow? The name sent a chill down my spine, a reminder of the darkness I was racing toward.

In an instant, my demeanor shifted. The vulnerability I had felt just moments before evaporated, replaced by a hardened determination. Every ounce of sorrow and self-doubt was pushed aside, buried beneath the instinct to chase justice. My heart raced, adrenaline flooding my veins, and I gripped the steering wheel tightly, the leather creaking under my fingers.

I couldn't afford to feel right now. I had to focus on the task ahead, to push through the emotions that threatened to drown me. I was a detective, a protector, and I wouldn't let my grief distract me from the work that needed to be done.

As the sirens wailed in the distance, growing louder with each passing second, I felt the familiar rush of purpose. I was on a mission now, and nothing would stand in my way. The asphalt road stretched out before me, a ribbon of black that twisted and turned, flanked by the skeletal silhouettes of trees that blurred into streaks of green and brown. Each curve sent adrenaline coursing through my veins, and I pressed down harder on the accelerator, the engine roaring in response as the car surged forward.

The world outside became a cacophony of colors—flashes of red brake lights, the dull gray of the pavement, and the occasional glint of sunlight reflecting off the windshields of passing cars. I was zipping past them, my heart pounding in sync with the rhythm of the tires gripping the road. The speedometer climbed higher, each tick marking the urgency

MIKEL WILSON

of my mission. I barely registered the speed limit as my mind raced, thoughts colliding in a chaotic swirl of images and fears.

What awaited me at the scene? What horrors had unfolded? My imagination spiraled into dark territories, conjuring grim scenarios: a body discarded like trash, a victim's last moments filled with terror. The Crow was out there, a malevolent force lurking in the shadows, and it was my job to bring that darkness into the light. Each passing second felt like an eternity, and I pushed myself to go faster, to reach the scene before more lives were shattered.

I could feel the tension coiling in my gut, a sickening knot that tightened with each mile. My mind raced with questions —*who was it this time? A mother, a sister, a friend?* I thought of the families left in the wake of this monster, their lives irrevocably changed by tragedy. I couldn't let fear consume me; I had to harness it, transform it into a relentless pursuit of justice.

The road blurred beneath me, each turn a reminder of the stakes at hand. I was no longer just a grieving woman; I was a detective, a guardian of the innocent, and I would not rest until the Crow was brought to justice. The sirens continued to wail, a haunting soundtrack to my mind, I pressed on, fueled by purpose and the desperate need to confront the nightmare that awaited me.

CHAPTER 12

NATALIE

I arrived at the crime scene, the sun barely peeking over the horizon, casting an eerie light upon the desolation. Officers were staking off places with yellow tape, their expressions grim and focused. I flashed my badge to gain access, my heart pounding as I saw Dom already there, crouched over his notepad, taking down his findings with meticulous precision.

"Morning, Detective," he said, nodding curtly. The tension between us was palpable, a lingering residue from the previous evening's argument. I deserved the animosity; I had been reckless, allowing my emotions to cloud my judgment.

I stepped closer, my eyes observing the gruesome scene while it unfolded before me. The body of a young girl lay sprawled across the burned earth, her skin an ash gray, a gunshot wound marring her chest. My stomach churned. *She*

MIKEL WILSON

was just a child, her life extinguished far too soon, her innocent dreams snuffed out by senseless violence. The acrid smell of burnt grass filled my nostrils, choking me, a visceral reminder of the horror that had transpired here. This was the work of our killer, the one we had been chasing—the Crow.

But there was something different about this scene. I knew of the other victims, but this girl—had they really gone so far as to leave a signature? In the corner of my mind, I wondered if it was a copycat. The media had been relentless, and somewhere among our ranks, there had to be a leak. The thought gnawed at me, feeding my anger and frustration.

"Did you know her?" Dom asked suddenly, breaking my reverie. His voice was soft, almost hesitant.

I shook my head, forcing myself to focus, to document the evidence. "No, but it doesn't matter. No one should die like this."

He looked at me, his eyes searching for mine. "It's okay to feel something. She was just a kid."

I felt a lump form in my throat. "It's not okay, Dom. We're supposed to protect them. And look what happened."

He didn't respond, his pen still scratching against the paper, but I could feel the weight of his silence pressing down on us. I took my pictures, forcing myself to focus, hoping the click of the camera would drown out the chaos in my mind. I requested forensics to use a drone to get aerial shots of the crime scene, hoping for a wider perspective that might reveal something we'd missed. As Dom finished compiling his findings, he carried them to his car, leaving me alone with the suffocating weight of despair.

Once back at the station, I walked over to his desk, my heart racing. I leaned in, whispering in his ear, "We need to talk."

He nodded, his expression unreadable, but I could see the

flicker of conflict in his eyes. We retreated to the break room, the fluorescent lights above casting a harsh glow on our tense silhouettes.

Taking a deep breath, I poured my heart out to him, my voice trembling as I recounted Marcus' murder—the guilt that clung to me like a shroud, the relentless haunting of my failures. "I thought I could save him, Dom. I thought I could stop it. And now..." My voice broke, a sob threatening to escape. "Now another innocent has died, and I feel like I'm losing control."

He placed his hand on my shoulder, grounding me, and then leaned in to kiss me softly, a connection that reminded me I wasn't alone in this darkness. "You aren't alone in this. You are my partner—both in life and in the field. I love you."

Just as the words settled between us, the break room started to fill with other officers, their chatter a stark contrast to the emotional turmoil swirling inside me. My phone rang, breaking the moment—a call from forensics.

"There is something you have to see," the voice on the other end said, urgency lacing their tone. "Come with me?"

Dom nodded, and we headed to the lab, the weight of dread pressing down on me. When we arrived, Abby, the head of forensics, looked up from her computer, her face a mask of concern. "You need to see this," she said, pulling up the footage captured by the drone.

The screen flickered to life, and my heart sank as I saw the scene from above. The body of the girl wasn't just lying on the burnt ground; it had been placed deliberately in the center of a giant burned crow, the charred outline of its wings extending around her like some grotesque altar.

"This took a lot of time and precision," Dom said, his voice low and filled with an unsettling mix of admiration and horror.

I felt my pulse quicken, anger surging through me. They

were getting cocky, too comfortable in their heinous acts. That cockiness would cost them—this much I knew. The need for justice burned inside me, a fervent fire igniting my very being.

"We have to bring them in," I said, my voice steady despite the chaos inside. "We can't let them get away with this. We can't let another innocent life be taken."

Abby nodded, her eyes wide with understanding. "We'll get everything we can from this. We need to analyze the crow's markings—it might lead us to something."

As we started discussing the next steps, my thoughts spiraled back to the girl. She had a name, a family, people who would mourn her. I could feel the weight of their grief, the emptiness left in their lives. The anger I felt was not just for the loss of life but for the pain it would inflict on those who loved her.

"I can't believe this is happening again," I said, my voice barely above a whisper, tears threatening to spill. "Why can't we stop it?"

Dom stepped closer, his presence a comforting balm against the storm of emotions raging within me. "We will stop it," he assured me, his voice low and steady. "We're not giving up. We'll find whoever did this, and we'll make them pay."

I looked into his eyes, searching for strength, for reassurance. "I can't lose anyone else, Dom. I can't bear it."

"You won't lose anyone," he vowed, his hand squeezing mine tightly. "We'll do this together. You and me against the world, remember?"

The strength in his voice ignited a tiny flicker of hope within me, and I nodded, feeling a surge of resolution he had given me strength. I would bring the killer to justice. I would not let fear and despair dictate my actions any longer. But as

I stood there, a new wave of anguish crashed over me—a realization that threatened to topple the shaky foundation I had just built.

That's when it hit me like a freight train. I needed to know who this girl was. I walked over to the missing persons wall, scanning the photographs that lined it like a heartbreaking gallery of lost innocence. Each face stared back at me, a silent plea for help etched into their features. After a moment that felt like an eternity, I found her. I pulled her picture off the wall, the weight of it heavy in my hands. Her name was Ellie. She was seventeen, the same age as my little sister.

I took a deep breath, fighting the lump forming in my throat. I could barely breathe as I called Dom over, my voice barely above a whisper. "I need you to contact her parents."

He nodded, sensing the gravity of the moment, but I barely registered his response. My eyes never left Ellie's face. In the picture, she was dressed in her cheerleader outfit, the purples and whites radiant against her flawless brown skin. Her black hair framed her face perfectly, and her smile was bright, infectious, a beacon of youth and joy. She had her whole life ahead of her, dreams and ambitions, friends and family who loved her. *And this is how she ended up?*

My mind flashed back to the graying corpse that lay in the sooty-filled grass, the horror of it clawing at my insides. I felt bile rise in my throat as the image of her lifeless body filled my vision, the way the sun had glinted off the terrible wound in her chest. My heart ached, a palpable pain that felt like a vice tightening around my chest.

Tears slipped unbidden down my cheeks, plopping onto Ellie's picture. I quickly wiped them away, ashamed of my weakness, but it was too late. The floodgates had opened, and the grief I had been holding back surged forth. I could see my little sister's face in Ellie's, her laughter echoing in my mind. How could this happen to a child? How could someone take away a life so vibrant, so full of potential?

CHAPTER 13

NATALIE

I felt rage boiling beneath the surface, a fiery anger that threatened to consume me. But deeper than that was the pain, the hurt—a visceral ache that clawed at my heart. I wanted to scream, to shout at the injustice of it all. This wasn't just a case; it wasn't just another statistic. This was a child, a beloved daughter, a friend.

With every beat of my heart, I could feel the pulse of her absence. What would her parents say when we told them? How could we even begin to explain that their baby girl was gone, snuffed out by the very darkness we were supposed to fight against? The thought of facing them, of looking into their grief-stricken eyes, made my heart race with fear and dread.

"Ellie," I whispered, my voice breaking. "I'm so sorry." I felt a desperate need to apologize to her, as if my words could somehow reach her, could somehow bring her back. I was a protector, a guardian in this world of chaos, and yet here I stood, powerless to save her.

I closed my eyes for a moment, trying to block out the world around me. I could hear the sounds of the precinct—the ringing phones, the murmurs of my colleagues, the clatter of keyboards—but all I could feel was the weight of sorrow pressing down on me. The grief was suffocating, like a thick fog that enveloped me, clouding my thoughts and choking my resolve.

"Why?" I asked the universe, the question hanging in the air like a dark cloud. *"Why her? Why now?"*

I opened my eyes and looked back at Ellie's picture, the bright smile that once lit up the world now a haunting reminder of what had been lost. The flicker of hope that had ignited moments ago was now overshadowed by despair. What could I possibly do to make sense of this? How could I fight against the darkness when it had already claimed an innocent life?

A sob escaped my lips, and I quickly turned away, ashamed of my vulnerability. I needed to be strong, to be the detective I was trained to be. But how could I focus on the case when my heart was breaking for this child?

"Dom," I called, my voice trembling. He turned to me, concern etched across his features. "What if we don't find the killer? What if they just keep hurting more children?"

His expression softened, and he stepped closer, placing a reassuring hand on my shoulder. "We will find them. We have to believe that. For Ellie. For her family."

But even as he spoke, doubt gnawed at me. I wanted to believe him, to let his words wash over me like a soothing balm. But the reality was too stark, too painful. I could see Ellie's face in every child I passed on the street, every laugh that echoed in the park. She was a victim, yes, but she was also a reminder—a reminder that we had to fight, that we had to protect those who couldn't protect themselves.

"Ellie," I whispered again, my heart breaking anew. "I promise you, I will not let your death be in vain. I will find the monster who did this to you."

I wiped my tears and took a deep breath, steadying myself. I could feel the fire of anger igniting within me once more, but this time, it was fueled by a sense of purpose. Ellie deserved justice, and I would do everything in my power to give it to her.

I turned away from the missing persons wall, I felt Dom's hand on my back, guiding me forward. Together, we would delve into the darkness, unearthing the truth and facing the horrors that lurked within. For Ellie. For every innocent life that had been lost and for every child that deserved to grow up free from fear. This was our mission now, and I would not falter. I would not let her memory fade into the shadows. I would fight for her, and I would make sure she was not forgotten.

Just then, a knock at the door interrupted our moment. Officer Grant stepped in, his face pale. "Sorry to interrupt, but we just got a call from the girl's parents. They want to speak to us. They're devastated."

I felt my heart drop. The thought of facing them, of looking into the eyes of a mother who would never hold her child again, was unbearable. "We can't," I said, shaking my head. "I can't do it."

Dom's grip tightened around my hand. "We owe it to her and her family to hear them out. They deserve answers."

My breath hitched in my throat. "But what can we possibly say? 'Sorry, we're doing our best, but it's not good enough'? How do we comfort them when we can't even comfort ourselves?"

"By being there," he said, his voice unwavering. "It's not

about having the right words. It's about showing them they're not alone in this. It's about letting them know we'll do everything we can to find their daughter's killer."

I hesitated, my heart racing. "What if they blame us?"

"Then they blame us," Dom replied, his gaze steady. "But we can't run from this. We have to face it together, just like we face everything else."

I took a deep breath, feeling the weight of his words sink in. He was right, of course. We couldn't hide from the consequences of our actions, nor could we shy away from the pain of the victims' families. "Okay," I whispered, my voice trembling. "Let's do it."

As we made our way to the conference room where the parents were waiting, I felt a churning in my stomach. *What could I possibly say to make this any better? How could I erase their grief, their anger, their heartbreak?*

When we entered, the atmosphere was thick with sorrow. The mother sat hunched over, her hair disheveled, tears streaming down her cheeks. The father gripped her hand tightly, his face etched with anguish. My heart ached for them, for the unimaginable pain they were experiencing.

"Detectives," the father said, his voice hoarse. "What do you know?"

I opened my mouth, but no words came out. All I could think about was the little girl, full of life and promise, now gone forever. "I'm so sorry for your loss," I finally managed, my voice quivering. "We're doing everything we can to find out who did this."

The mother looked up, her eyes red and swollen. "You don't understand! She was just a child! She was... she was my baby!" Her voice broke, and she buried her face in her hands, sobs wracking her body.

I felt as though I had been punched in the gut. I wanted to reach out and comfort her, but I was paralyzed by the weight of my own inadequacy. "I know—" I began, but the words felt hollow.

"We're so sorry," Dom interjected gently, stepping forward. "We promise you won't be alone in this. We will find the person responsible. We will bring them to justice."

The father looked up, anger flashing in his eyes. "Justice? What does that even mean? You think that will bring her back? You think that will fix this?"

I braced myself for his words, feeling the sting of his rage. "No," I said softly, holding his gaze. "I don't think it will. But that's all we can do. We owe it to her to find the truth, to make sure no one else suffers like this."

The mother's cries filled the room, and I felt my heart shatter. I could see the pain etched on their faces, the devastation that would haunt them for the rest of their lives. I wanted to offer them something—anything—that would ease their suffering, but I was powerless.

"Please," the mother said, her voice trembling. "Please find whoever did this. I can't bear the thought of them still out there, free to hurt others."

"We will," I vowed, tears streaming down my cheeks. "We promise. We won't stop until we do."

As we left the room, I felt the weight of their grief pressing down on me like a heavy shroud. That little girl wasn't just a victim; she was a daughter, a sister, a friend. She had dreams, hopes, and a future that had been stolen from her. And in that moment, I vowed to honor her memory by bringing her killer to justice.

Dom's hand found mine as we stepped into the hallway, and I looked up at him, my heart heavy with sorrow. "What if we don't find them?" I whispered, my voice breaking.

"We will," he said firmly, pulling me close. "We have to believe that. For her sake. For her parents' sake."

As the sun began to set, casting long shadows along the

MIKEL WILSON

pavement, I felt a renewed determination within me. I would not let the darkness win. I would fight for that little girl, for all the innocent lives taken too soon. We would find the Crow, and we would make them pay.

And in the depths of my despair, I found a flicker of hope —the hope that justice could still be served, that we could bring light into the darkness. The Crow would go down and I would make sure of it, no matter what. After all of that, I needed to see my baby sister. Maybe seeing Mackinzie would help.

"Dom, how would you feel about me inviting Mackinzie over? She messaged me about a boyfriend she wanted me to meet. Maybe this could take my mind off of everything."

"Baby of course, plus Mackinzie is growing up on us I may have to put her new boyfriend in a headlock." he joked while flexing his rippling muscles.

I picked up my phone and dialed Mackenzie's number, my heart racing with anticipation. As the phone rang, I could hear her laughter on the other end before she even answered.

"How's tonight?" I asked, a smile creeping onto my face.

"Perfect! I just finished my homework, and I'm ready to hang out. I'll call him right now, and we'll be right over. Love you, big sister!" she replied, her enthusiasm infectious.

"Okay, everything is set," I said, feeling a warmth spread through me. "Want to order a few pizzas? You know her; she'll eat anything—well, mostly anything," I laughed, picturing Mackenzie's picky yet adventurous eating habits.

"Absolutely! I can't wait to see her face when she arrives. What do you want?" Dom chimed in, glancing over at me with that familiar playful grin.

"How about pepperoni and extra cheese for me? And maybe a veggie for Mackenzie?" I suggested, knowing she often tried to eat healthier, even if she occasionally indulged in the cheesy goodness of pizza.

"Got it!" Dom said, already reaching for his phone to place the order. "I'll add a large Hawaiian for good measure. Can't go wrong with a little pineapple, right?"

I raised an eyebrow playfully. "You and your pineapple obsession. I'll never understand it, but if it keeps you happy, go for it!"

As he dialed the pizza place, I headed to my room to change. I rummaged through my closet and pulled out a faded black skull t-shirt, a favorite of mine, and paired it with a flowing black skirt that swished around my knees. I glanced in the mirror, feeling a little more like myself— something I desperately needed after the chaos of the day.

"Do I look okay?" I called out to Dom, who was still on the phone.

"More than okay! You look amazing," he replied, his voice warm and sincere. "I'll tell the pizza guy to hurry up; I can't wait to see your sister's face when she walks in."

I chuckled, imagining Mackenzie's excited expression. "She's going to be so hyper, you know that, right? It's like she's on a sugar rush just from the thought of pizza."

"Hey, it's not just the pizza; it's the quality sister time too," Dom said, finally finishing his order. "Three large pizzas, one pepperoni and extra cheese, one veggie, and a Hawaiian. Should be here in about thirty minutes!"

"Perfect timing!" I said, feeling a rush of excitement. I walked back into the living room, where Dom was finishing up. "Now we just need to find something to watch while we wait."

"Any suggestions? I can't let you pick another rom-com," he teased, crossing his arms and giving me a mock-serious look.

"Oh come on! Rom-coms are classics!" I shot back, rolling my eyes but unable to suppress a grin. "How about we compromise and watch that new thriller? You know, the one where there's a tornado and the dumb people are chasing it, not running away?"

"Fine, but only if you promise to keep the lights on," he laughed, his eyes sparkling with mischief.

"Deal!" I said, feeling grateful for these moments of laughter and connection. As we settled onto the couch, I felt a sense of peace wash over me, knowing my sister would be here soon, and together, we'd share laughter, stories, and, of course, pizza.

CHAPTER 14

NATALIE

The door swung open, and in walked Mackinzie, her face lit up with excitement. Her dirty blonde hair bounced with each step, framing her pale face, and her black glasses perched on her nose gave her a studious charm. Right behind her was Kel, her boyfriend—a stocky guy with dark brown skin and a slightly awkward demeanor, wearing a graphic tee that looked a size too big. He gave me a shy smile, but there was something unsettling about it that I couldn't quite put my finger on.

"Hey, big sis!" Mackinzie exclaimed, practically bouncing on her toes. "I brought Kel! I hope that's okay!"

"Of course," I replied, forcing a smile even as a knot tightened in my stomach. I could feel Dom's eyes on me, sensing my unease. "We just ordered pizza. You two hungry?"

"Starving!" Mackinzie said, practically bouncing toward the couch. "Kel's been talking about pizza all day!" Just when she said that a knock at the door echoed through the house.

Pizza! Mackinzie said with a smile. Dom walked over to the door and paid the delivery man and then placed the pizza on the table.

As we settled in, the smell of freshly baked pizza wafted through the air, a tantalizing mix of melted cheese and spicy pepperoni. I could almost taste it as I reached for a slice, my stomach growling in anticipation. But my attention was diverted as I glanced at Kel. Something about him was off, and I couldn't shake the feeling that I'd seen him before.

"Kel, what do you do?" I asked, trying to keep my voice light.

"Oh, uh, I'm studying computer science," he said, adjusting his glasses with slightly trembling fingers. "And I work part-time at a tech store. You know, fixing stuff."

"Sounds interesting," I replied, but the knot in my stomach tightened. I couldn't shake the nagging feeling. And then it hit me—Kel's face flickered in my mind, a flashing image from a recent news report about a criminal on the run for writing bad checks. My heart raced.

"Wait a minute," I said, my voice sharp. "Your last name isn't… it can't be…"

Mackinzie's expression shifted as she looked from me to Kel, confusion clouding her features. "What do you mean?"

"Kel, are you on the most wanted list?" I asked, my voice growing louder. "Because if you are, you're not just some kid working at a tech store!"

"What? No!" Kel stammered, his eyes wide. "That's not me! I swear!"

I stood up, pacing in front of them, the smell of pizza fading into the background. "Then why does your face look so familiar? You know what? I don't need to ask. You're the guy who's been writing bad checks and getting arrested!"

Mackinzie's face fell. "You can't be serious! Kel wouldn't do that!"

"Wouldn't do what?" I shot back, my voice rising. "He's a criminal, Mackinzie! You're dating a criminal!"

"Stop it!" she yelled, her voice breaking. "You don't know him like I do! He's a good guy!"

"A good guy who's wanted by the police!" I snapped, my heart racing. "You can't be serious right now."

Dom stood up, sensing the escalating tension. "Maybe we should all just take a breath," he suggested, trying to defuse the situation. "Let's eat, watch a movie, and talk this out."

But I wasn't having it. "No! I can't just ignore this. I'm a cop, Mackinzie. I can't let this slide!"

"Just because you're a cop doesn't mean you can dictate my life!" she shouted back, tears welling in her eyes.

"Your life? You're dating a criminal! I can't just stand by and let this happen!" I felt the heat rising in my chest, a mix of anger and protectiveness.

"Maybe I don't need you to protect me!" she shot back, her voice trembling with anger. "I can make my own choices!"

"Choices? This isn't just a choice, Mackenzie. This is dangerous!" I exclaimed, my frustration boiling over. "You have no idea what he's capable of!"

Kel shifted uncomfortably, glancing between us, his face paling as the tension thickened. "I didn't do anything wrong. I swear!" he pleaded. "It was a misunderstanding!"

I couldn't take it anymore. "I'll prove it!" I said, my voice steady with resolve. I turned and marched towards my room, my heart pounding in my chest. "I'll get my badge and my gun, and I'll arrest you right now!"

I could hear Mackinzie's voice following me, panic lacing her words. "You can't do this! You're going to ruin everything!"

I ignored her, retrieving my badge and my gun from the drawer, the cold metal feeling heavy in my hands. This was my job, my duty. I couldn't let my feelings for my sister cloud my judgment.

When I returned to the living room, Kel stood up, a look of defiance on his face. "You're not going to arrest me," he said, his voice shaky but strong.

"Oh, I am," I replied, my voice firm. "You're coming with me."

As I moved to cuff him, he suddenly lunged at me, and I reacted instinctively, slamming his face onto the coffee table. The sound echoed in the room, and I could hear Mackinzie gasp behind me.

"Kel!" she shouted, rushing forward, but I held him down firmly.

"You're not going to resist!" I growled, feeling adrenaline surge through me. "You're wanted, and you need to face the consequences!"

"Why are you doing this?" Kel yelled, struggling beneath me. "Mackinzie set me up! This is all her fault!"

"Shut up!" I snapped, my anger flaring. "Don't you dare blame her for your choices!"

Mackinzie stepped back, her face pale, tears streaming down her cheeks. "I didn't set him up! I love him!"

"Love him? You're in love with a criminal!" I shouted, my frustration boiling over. "How can you not see how dangerous this is?"

"Stop it! Just stop!" she cried, her voice breaking. "You're tearing us apart!"

I heard the sirens approaching in the distance, the sound filling me with a sense of relief and dread. I was doing what I had to do, but the thought of hurting my sister in the process gnawed at me.

When the other officers arrived, they quickly took Kel into custody, his protests fading into the background as they

FLAMES OF THE CROWS BETRAYAL

led him away. Mackinzie stood frozen in place, her expression a mix of shock and heartbreak.

"Why did you have to call it in?" I asked, frustration bubbling within me as I turned to her. "You didn't have to do that!"

"Because I didn't know what else to do!" she shouted back, her voice trembling with rage. "You were about to hurt him, and I didn't want you to ruin everything!"

Dom stepped in, trying to mediate. "Mackenzie, he's a criminal. You can't expect her to just look the other way."

"Maybe I don't want to be part of this!" she yelled, her voice rising. "You think you can just control my life because you're a cop? You think this is easy for me?"

"I'm trying to protect you!" I exclaimed, my heart racing. "You're my sister, and I can't stand the thought of you being with someone like him!"

She shook her head, tears spilling down her cheeks. "You don't get to decide that for me! I love him, and you just ruined everything!"

Without another word, she turned on her heel and stormed out of the apartment, slamming the door behind her. The sound echoed in the silence that followed, leaving a heavy weight in the air.

Dom looked at me, disappointment etched across his face. "You didn't have to go that far," he said quietly. "You could have handled it differently."

I felt a surge of anger at his words. "He's a criminal, Dom! I had to arrest him. I'm a cop first!"

"But what about Mackinzie?" he pressed, his voice steady. "You just pushed her away. You didn't have to call it in!"

I felt my heart sink as I realized the truth in his words. "I was just trying to protect her."

"And now she's gone," Dom said softly, shaking his head.

"You need to think about how this affects your family, not just your job."

I fumed, my emotions swirling in a tempest of anger and regret. *I cared about my sister more than anything, but I couldn't let a criminal put her in danger. I had done what I thought was right,* but now I felt a crushing sense of loss.

Dom left through the door, the weight of his words hung in the air like a thick fog.

"Just think hard about what matters most, your job or your family," his tone a mix of urgency and frustration. I felt a jolt of anger rise within me, and I cut my eyes at him, watching as he disappeared out of the house.

The door swung shut with a loud thud, leaving me in an oppressive silence. My heart raced as Dom's words echoed in my mind, reverberating like a drumbeat of doubt. I turned away from the door, my heart heavy with the conflict swirling inside me.

"What does he know?" I muttered under my breath, running a hand through my hair in frustration. "He doesn't understand the pressure I'm under."

I looked around the empty room, the walls adorned with pictures of laughter, joy, and moments I had almost forgotten. There was a photo of Mackinzie, at her sixth birthday, her face smeared with cake and grinning from ear to ear. I could almost hear her laughter, a sound that used to fill our home. Our mother had died later that year and all she had was me.

Standing there alone, I could feel the weight of my choices which hung heavy in the air, a reminder that sometimes, doing the right thing meant losing the people you loved. I had to balance my duty with my heart, but for now, all I felt was the sting of betrayal and the emptiness of an apartment that had once been filled with laughter.

CHAPTER 15

DOM

I returned to the apartment, a sense of dread washed over me. The door creaked open, revealing the dimly lit living room where Natalie sat on the couch, her arms crossed tightly over her chest. Her brow was furrowed, and her lips formed a pout that made my heart sink. It was a familiar sight—one that pulled at my heartstrings and ignited a fire of frustration within me.

"Hey," I said softly, stepping further into the room. The air felt heavy between us, thick with unspoken words. I took a deep breath, mustering the courage to bridge the chasm that had formed between us.

Natalie didn't respond, her gaze fixed on the floor as if it held the answers to everything. I sighed and sat down beside her, the couch sinking slightly under my weight. The tension was palpable, and for a moment, the silence stretched out, a taut string ready to snap.

"Natalie," I began, my voice gentle yet firm. "I know

things have been tough lately, but we can't let this job consume us. It's not everything. You… you mean more to me than any paycheck ever could." I took her hand, hoping to feel a flicker of warmth against my palm, but she pulled away slightly, her eyes still cast downward.

"I just don't understand, Dom," she finally said, her voice barely above a whisper. "You're always working late, always trying to climb that ladder. What about us? What about our life together?"

"I'm doing it for us!" I exclaimed, my frustration bubbling to the surface. "I want to build a future for us, to give you everything you deserve! But I can't do that if I'm not working hard. I want to settle down, I want to marry you! You're my everything, Natalie."

With that, I reached into my pocket, my heart pounding as I pulled out a small, velvet ring case. I placed it on the table between us, the soft click of the lid echoing in the quiet room. Her eyes flicked to the case, a mixture of surprise and uncertainty flashing across her features.

"Dom…" she started, her voice trembling.

I watched as she took a deep breath, her expression shifting from shock to something more guarded. "Is this… is this what I think it is?"

"Open it," I urged, my heart racing. "I want you to know how serious I am about us. I want to be with you, Natalie. I want to build a life together—a family."

But instead of reaching for the ring, she stood up abruptly, her chair scraping against the floor in a harsh, grating sound. "I can't do this right now!" she exclaimed, her voice rising in anger and frustration. "You don't get it! You think a ring will fix everything? You think this is just about a commitment? It's not! It's about you being here, in the moment, with me!"

I felt my heart shatter as she turned and walked away, her

FLAMES OF THE CROWS BETRAYAL

footsteps echoing in the emptiness of the room. "Natalie, please!" I called after her, desperation creeping into my voice. "Don't walk away from this. Don't walk away from us!"

But she didn't stop. She disappeared down the hallway, leaving me alone with my thoughts and the heavy silence that enveloped the apartment. The weight of her words pressed down on me, suffocating and raw.

Heartbroken and angry, I stormed out of the apartment, the door slamming shut behind me. I stumbled down the stairs and into my car, my hands gripping the steering wheel so tightly that my knuckles turned white. I needed to escape, to clear my head, so I drove aimlessly, the streets blurring past me until I found myself at the lake.

The moon hung low in the sky, casting a silvery glow over the still water. I parked the car and stepped out, the cool breeze wrapping around me like a comforting blanket. I walked to the edge of the lake, the soft crunch of gravel beneath my feet the only sound in the stillness of the night.

As I stood there, gazing out over the water, memories flooded my mind. I thought of my father, the man I had never known. He had walked out on my mother when she was pregnant with me, leaving her to raise me alone. The pain of abandonment coursed through my veins like a poison, a reminder of what I had lost before I even had a chance to gain it.

What kind of father leaves? What kind of man walks away from his family? The questions swirled around in my mind like the ripples on the surface of the lake, taunting me with their unanswered truths.

I thought of Natalie, of her laughter and warmth, the way her eyes sparkled when she talked about her dreams. I couldn't bear the thought of losing her, of repeating the cycle of abandonment that had haunted my family for generations. I *didn't want to be like my father. I wanted to be there for her, to build a life together, to create a family filled with love and laughter.*

But what if I couldn't? What if my job consumed me, just like it had consumed so many before me? My heart raced with anxiety as I crouched down at the water's edge, my fingers skimming the surface of the lake. The coolness sent a shiver through me, a stark contrast to the heat of my frustration and fear.

I refuse to give up on her, on us, I would do anything to make it work with Natalie. I want to be the man she deserves, the father I never had the chance to be.

As the moonlight danced across the water, it cast a silvery sheen that shimmered like diamonds on the lake's surface. I stood frozen, the cool breeze washing over me, momentarily soothing the tempest within my heart. With my eyes closed, I let the wind wrap around me, hoping it could carry away my anguish. In my mind's eye, I envisioned a life filled with joy—Natalie beside me, laughter echoing through our home, children running in the yard, their tiny feet pattering against the ground. I could almost hear their laughter, sweet and innocent, and feel the warmth of their small arms wrapping around me in joyful embraces.

But then, reality crashed over me like a wave, pulling me back into the depths of despair. *How do I make her see?* The weight of my fear pressing down hard on my chest, tightening like a vice. The thought of her disappointment was suffocating. Tears began to pool in my eyes, blurring my vision as they spilled down my cheeks, warm trails of sorrow that I could no longer contain.

I can't lose her, I won't let my past dictate my future. My heart ached with the knowledge that I had been given a chance to build something beautiful, something real, but even now, it felt like it was slipping through my fingers like grains of sand. I could feel my dreams, my hopes for a family, my visions of laughter and love, dissolving into the darkness of doubt.

The air was thick with emotion, each breath I took was heavy with the weight of what was at stake. I stood up, my legs shaky beneath me, but resolve surged through my veins. I had to fight for what mattered most. I turned my gaze back to the lake, the moon's reflection shimmering like a beacon of hope amidst my turmoil.

I'll do whatever it takes, each word a desperate plea to the universe. *I'll show her that I can be different. I can be the man she needs.*

I took a deep breath, the cool night air filling my lungs, but it did little to ease the suffocating pressure of my heartache. I could feel the tears continuing to fall, now mingling with the chill of the breeze, as I thought of Natalie's face—the way her eyes sparkled when she smiled, the way her laughter lit up even the darkest corners of my soul. The thought of losing that light made me feel as if the ground was crumbling beneath my feet.

I know I'm not perfect, tears blurring my vision as *But I want to be better. I want to show her that I can change, that I can be present, that I can give her everything she deserves.* The ache in my chest intensified, a raw, visceral pain that felt like it was tearing me apart from the inside. My dreams were slipping away, and I could do nothing but stand there, helpless, as the vision of our future faded into darkness.

I made my way back to the car, each step felt like a monumental effort. My heart still ached, but the despair was now intertwined with an ember of determination. I wanted to redefine my destiny, to prove to Natalie—and to myself— that love was worth fighting for. I climbed into the car, the familiar scent of leather and gasoline bringing me back to reality, but my heart felt heavy.

I started the engine, the sound echoing into the stillness

of the night. It was a reminder that life continued, even when it felt like everything was falling apart. I drove back to the apartment, my mind racing with thoughts of how to make her understand, how to show her that my heart was hers, now and forever.

The tears continued to fall, each one a reminder of my fear, my love, and my desperation to hold onto the life I had dreamed of. *Please, let her see, I'm willing to fight, to change, to be the man she deserves.*

As the familiar buildings of our neighborhood came into view, I felt a swell of hope rising within me, pushing against the sorrow that threatened to overwhelm me. *I couldn't give up—not on Natalie, not on the family I longed to create. I would confront my fears, lay bare my heart, and fight for the love that had once felt so secure. I would not let my past define me; instead, I would rise from the ashes of my own doubts, ready to reclaim what was rightfully mine.*

CHAPTER 16

DOM

The house was eerily quiet when I arrived home, the only sound was the faint ticking of the wall clock that seemed to mock my turmoil with each passing second. I stepped inside, the door creaking softly as it shut behind me. The emptiness wrapped around me like a suffocating blanket, a stark reminder of the distance that had grown between Natalie and me. She was probably at the precinct, buried in a case that had taken over her life. And while I knew better than to cause a scene, I couldn't shake the feeling that I needed to confront her. I needed to fix this —whatever "this" was.

I sank into the worn-out armchair in the living room, the fabric rough against my skin. Gazing out the window, I watched the first rays of sunlight pierce the horizon, illuminating the world outside in a soft, golden glow. But within me, darkness loomed. Thoughts of her nightmares haunted me, the way she would wake up screaming, drenched in sweat, the terror etched into her features. The guilt twisted like a knife in my gut. I was supposed to protect her, to be her rock, yet I felt more like a shadow lurking in the background.

As the sun rose higher, I finally forced myself to get up. I fixed a cup of coffee, the rich aroma filling the air, a small comfort in my otherwise tumultuous mind. I changed into clean clothes, each movement mechanical, my mind racing with thoughts of how I would address the chaos that had become our lives. I couldn't just sit back and let the distance grow any longer. Tomorrow, I would crash her therapy session. I would confront her, face the demons that haunt us both, and somehow, I would make her understand that I was here for her.

The next morning, I drove to the therapist's office, my heart pounding in my chest. I parked outside, anxiety coiling in my stomach as I watched the building standing before me. The world felt so normal, so unaware of the storm brewing inside me. I took a deep breath, steeling myself for what I was about to do. I had no idea how Natalie would react, but I was determined to show her that I was willing to fight for us.

I stepped into the office, the smell of lavender and chamomile wafting through the air, an attempt at creating a calming atmosphere. The therapist, a middle-aged woman with kind eyes, looked up as I entered. "Oh, Dom," she said, a hint of surprise in her voice. "I didn't expect to see you here." I looked into her eyes and her desk with her little bell. I wonder how much progress she had made or if Natalie had even told her about what she had done.

"Yeah, well, neither did I, but..." My voice trailed off as I spotted Natalie sitting across from her, her arms crossed tightly over her chest, her expression a mix of defiance and vulnerability. The sight of her sent a rush of emotions surging through me—love, anger, fear—all tangled together like a chaotic knot.

"Dom, what are you doing here?" Natalie's voice was sharp, her eyes narrowing as they met mine.

"I came to talk," I said, my tone steady, though my heart raced. "About you. About what you're going through."

Natalie scoffed, rolling her eyes. "This isn't your place,Dom. This is my session."

"Is it really? Because it seems to me that you're struggling, and I can't just stand by and watch you suffer alone," I replied, my frustration bubbling to the surface.

The therapist interjected, her calm demeanor faltering slightly. "Dom, maybe it's best if you let Natalie speak for herself. This is her safe space."

I shot her a look, my patience wearing thin. "Safe space? What about my space? What about the home we've built together? I can't just pretend everything is okay while you're fighting demons in your head!"

Natalie's face tightened, her lips pursed in anger. "You don't know anything about my demons, Dom! You think this is easy for me? You think I want to wake up every night screaming? You think I want to feel like I'm losing my mind?"

"I just want to help!" I exclaimed, my voice rising. "But you keep pushing me away. I'm trying to reach you, but it's like you're in a different world, and I can't break through!"

As the tension in the room escalated, I felt the air grow thicker, suffocating me with its weight. Natalie's expression hardened, and I could see the walls she had built around herself rising higher. "You don't get it, do you? You never have! You think this is just about me being 'weak' or 'crazy'? This is about survival!"

Before I could respond, I watched her reach into her bag,

MIKEL WILSON

my heart racing as dread clawed its way up my throat. Time seemed to slow as I realized what she was pulling out. My breath caught in my chest, the world around me fading into a blur as she unveiled her service weapon, the metal glinting ominously under the harsh fluorescent lights of the therapist's office. The sight of it struck a primal fear deep within me, sending adrenaline coursing through my veins. "What are you doing?" I shouted, my voice cracking, a mixture of fear and anger colliding within me as I instinctively took a step back, my body screaming for distance.

"Don't come any closer!" she yelled, her eyes wide with a mix of fear and rage, like a cornered animal ready to strike. The gun trembled slightly in her grip, reflecting the turmoil churning inside her. "You think you can just barge in here and fix everything? You can't! You have no idea what I go through every single day. You don't know what it's like to carry this weight!"

Each word felt like a dagger, sharp and piercing, cutting through the fragile facade of our relationship. I could see the pain etched across her face, the tension in her jaw, the way her hands shook as she fought to maintain control. It was as if the weapon in her hand symbolized the battles she fought daily—the nightmares that haunted her, the memories she couldn't escape. I wanted to reach out, to tell her that I understood, that I was here to help her shoulder that burden, but the distance between us felt insurmountable at that moment.

"Please, Natalie," I pleaded, my voice softening, trying to penetrate the chaos enveloping us. "You don't need to do this. I'm not your enemy. I want to help you, but you have to let me in." My heart raced, not just from fear of the gun but from the fear of losing her, of watching her slip away into a darkness I couldn't reach.

Her eyes flickered with uncertainty, the mask of anger slipping just enough for me to see the vulnerability beneath. "You don't know what you're asking," she spat, her voice trembling. "You don't know what I've seen, what I've done to survive. I can't let you in. I can't let anyone in."

The intensity of the moment hung heavy in the air, charged with emotion. The silence that followed felt deafening, a chasm between us filled with unspoken fears and aching love. Every fiber of my being screamed to close that distance, to bridge the gap and pull her back from the brink. All I wanted was to reach her, to show her that she didn't have to carry this weight alone. But how could I when she was so fiercely determined to keep me out?

The therapist's face paled, panic flickering in her eyes. "Natalie, let's just take a breath," she urged, her voice shaking slightly. "There's no need for this. I'm going to call the police if you don't calm down."

At that moment, a surge of frustration boiled over. "We are the police!" I snapped, the absurdity of the situation hitting me like a ton of bricks. The words hung in the air, and for a split second, the tension dissipated, replaced by a shared moment of incredulity. Both Natalie and I exchanged a bewildered look, and then, unexpectedly, laughter erupted between us, breaking through the storm of emotions.

"Seriously?" Natalie said, her voice still trembling but now tinged with disbelief. "We're the police?"

"Yeah, two broken cops in a therapist's office," I said, shaking my head as a breathless chuckle escaped my lips. "What a cliché."

It was a brief moment of levity, a flicker of connection amidst the chaos, but as quickly as it came, the gravity of our situation crashed back down. Natalie's laughter faded, replaced by a heavy silence. She lowered the weapon slightly,

MIKEL WILSON

the anger in her eyes replaced by something softer—fear, perhaps, or vulnerability.

"Dom," she said, her voice barely above a whisper. "I don't want this to be our life. I don't want to feel this way anymore."

"I don't want that either," I replied, my heart aching for her. "But we can't ignore it. You're not alone in this. I'm here. I want to help you fight, but you have to let me in."

Her gaze shifted from the weapon to me, confusion and pain written across her features. Slowly, she placed the gun back in her bag, the tension in the room still thick but slightly more manageable. The therapist breathed a sigh of relief, her demeanor shifting back to one of calm professionalism.

"Okay," the therapist said gently, her tone soothing. "Let's take a moment to breathe, and then we can talk about how we can work through this as a team. Together."

I could feel Natalie's eyes on me, searching for something —perhaps reassurance or understanding. I took a step closer, my heart pounding as I reached for her hand. "We'll figure this out, I promise," I said, my voice a low whisper. "We'll fight together."

Tears welled in her eyes, and she squeezed my hand tightly, the warmth of her touch grounding me amidst the chaos. "I don't want to be scared anymore," she admitted, her voice trembling.

"You don't have to be," I replied, my heart swelling with determination. "I'm right here. We're going to face this. Together."

And as we sat there, hand in hand, surrounded by the remnants of our argument and the weight of our struggles, I realized that while the path ahead would be challenging, we wouldn't have to walk it alone. We would confront our fears, fight for each other, and somehow, we would find a way to heal.

Listen, you go home and take some time to yourself and I will get a room or something and we can talk after we have both calmed down.

CHAPTER 17

NATALIE

I sat on the edge of my bed, my heart heavy with the weight of the previous night's confrontation. Dom had decided to stay somewhere I guess to get his thoughts together. The walls of my apartment felt like they were closing in on me, each breath a reminder of the unresolved tension with Dom. I had overreacted; I knew that now. The stress of the case, the sleepless nights filled with nightmares, and the constant pressure of my job had taken their toll. I needed to fix things with him, to reach out and mend what had been broken. But as I sat there, a pit of anxiety twisted in my stomach, making it hard to think straight.

Just then, my phone buzzed on the nightstand, shattering the suffocating silence. I picked it up, my heart racing, hoping it was Dom reaching out. But the name on the screen sent a jolt of fear through me. It was Mackinzie, my baby sister. I answered, a sense of dread pooling in my chest.

"Mackinzie?" I said, trying to keep my voice steady. But the sound of her sobs on the other end shattered my composure.

"Natalie! Please, help me!" Her voice was frantic, panicked, and the fear in her tone sent chills racing down my spine. "He's going to kill me!"

"Mackinzie, where are you? What's happening?" I demanded, my heart dropping to the floor as her words sank in.

"I'm at my apartment! He's here! Please, I'm so scared!" Her voice trembled, and I could hear the sound of glass shattering in the background, a crash that echoed like a gunshot in my ears.

"Mackinzie, stay on the line! I'm coming!" I shouted, adrenaline surging through me as I bolted out of bed. I grabbed my keys and raced out the door, my heart pounding a frantic rhythm against my ribs.

The drive to her apartment felt like a blur, each second stretching into an eternity. I could barely focus on the road, my mind racing with terrifying scenarios. *What if I was too late? What if I couldn't save her?* The thought clawed at my insides, filling me with an overwhelming sense of dread. I could see her face, her bright smile, the way she looked at the world with a mix of innocence and courage. *How could someone want to hurt her?*

I pulled into the parking lot, the familiar building loomed before me like a dark omen. I jumped out of my car, my heart racing as I sprinted towards the entrance. I could hear the faint echoes of her screams bouncing off the walls, each one a dagger to my heart. "Mackinzie!" I shouted, urgency fueling my steps.

I reached her apartment door, panic flooding my senses as I fumbled with the handle, my heart pounding so hard I thought it might burst from my chest. The door was locked, but I could hear the chaos unfolding inside—her desperate cries for help, punctuated by the sound of fists striking flesh.

"Mackinzie!" I cried again, pounding on the door. "Open up! I'm coming in!"

With no time to waste, I kicked the door hard, adrenaline giving me the strength I needed. The door broke open with a splintering crack, and I stumbled into the room, my eyes wide with horror.

What I saw stopped me cold. Mackinzie was backed against the wall, her boyfriend, Kel, was towering over her, his fists raised. Blood dripped from her mouth, staining her shirt, and the sight of it ignited a firestorm of rage within me.

"Get away from her!" I shouted, charging forward without thinking. At that moment, it was all instinct; I couldn't let him hurt her any further. I tackled him to the ground, the impact jarring my body as I wrestled with him.

"Get off me, you psycho!" he yelled, flinging me off like I was nothing. I scrambled to my feet, my heart racing as I lunged at him again. But he was faster. In a moment of sheer desperation, he pulled out a knife, its blade glinting menacingly in the dim light.

"Mackinzie, get out of here!" I screamed, panic seizing my chest as I saw the fear in her eyes. But she was frozen, unable to move, her gaze locked onto the chaos unfolding before her.

Before I could react, Kel lunged at me, the knife plunging into my side with a sharp, agonizing pain that stole my breath. I gasped, feeling warmth spreading across my shirt, the realization of what had just happened crashing down on me like a wave.

The world around me slowed, the sounds of Mackinzie's cries fading into the background. I felt a surge of adrenaline, a primal urge to protect my sister overriding everything else. With a burst of strength, I grabbed his wrist and twisted, forcing him to drop the knife. It clattered to the floor, but before I could catch my breath, I knew it was now or never.

I pulled my gun from its holster, aiming it at him, my hands shaking not just from the pain but from the weight of what I was about to do. "Get away from her!" I shouted, my voice trembling but fierce.

"Mackinzie, get back!" I yelled as Kel lunged at me again, his face twisted in rage. Without thinking, I pulled the trigger. The sound echoed in the small apartment, a deafening crack that shattered the chaos. He dropped to the ground, lifeless, the shock of what I had done crashing over me like a cold wave.

"Mackinzie!" I turned to her, panic flooding my veins as I rushed to her side. She was shaking, tears streaming down her face, her voice a choked sob.

"You didn't have to kill him!" she cried, her eyes wide with a mix of horror and disbelief.

"I had to protect you!" I shouted back, my voice strained. But as I looked at her battered and bruised face and busted lip, the pain in my side intensified, a burning fire that spread through my body. I felt myself sway, the world around me beginning to blur as darkness crept in at the edges of my vision.

"Mackinzie, I need you to call for help!" I gasped, my voice barely a whisper. The room spun around me, and I could feel my knees giving way. I collapsed to the floor, my vision fading, the last thing I heard was her frantic voice, calling for help, the sound echoing in my ears as everything went black.

As I drifted into unconsciousness, the last thought that crossed my mind was a desperate hope that I hadn't been too late to save my sister. I woke up in an ambulance. They had oxygen on my face while they rushed me to the hospital. I

MIKEL WILSON

looked over to see a sobbing Mackinzie. "You killed him."
And he tried to kill you, I don't know what to feel anymore."

"Sis I'm here for you, you didn't deserve that." Her bruised
face and busted nose made me forget about the pain of the
stab. My eyes filled with tears at the fact that I nearly just lost
my sister. When a sharp pain in my side caused my body to
shake. The paramedics rushed over to me and slowly the
darkness overtook me.

CHAPTER 18

DOM

The phone rang incessantly, a shrill, relentless sound that pierced through the thick fog of my thoughts. I didn't want to hear it. I didn't want to hear anything that could confirm the sinking realization that our relationship was crumbling, that Natalie didn't want me anymore. I sat in silence at the motel, the weight of despair pressing down on my chest like a heavy stone. I had ignored her calls, letting them go to voicemail, each ring a reminder of the distance that had grown between us. I was torn up and sad but every part of me wanted to go home. *But what would that change?*

Finally, I picked up the phone, my heart racing as I saw I had thirty unread voicemail messages. My stomach twisted into knots as I clicked on the first one. Mackinzie's voice broke through, raw and filled with anguish, "Call me, Dom. It's about Natalie."

At that moment, my heart seemed to drop into an abyss, a

MIKEL WILSON

cold fear wrapping around me like a vise. I knew something was wrong. I dialed her number back, my hands shaking uncontrollably. The moment she answered, I could barely recognize her through her sobs. "Dom, it's Natalie... she's been stabbed... she's in surgery."

The world around me began to spin, the walls closing in as I ran out the door, the cold air hitting my face like a slap. I jumped into my car, pressing the accelerator hard against the floor. The engine roared to life, and I drove as fast as the car would allow, my mind racing faster than the speedometer could measure. Every second felt like an eternity, my heart pounding loud enough to drown out the sound of the tires screeching against the pavement.

When I arrived at the hospital, the fluorescent lights buzzed overhead, casting a harsh glare that made my heart race even faster. I stumbled through the automatic doors, the sterile smell of antiseptic and fear flooding my senses. My breath came in short gasps as I approached the reception desk, desperation clawing at my throat. "Where is she? Where's Natalie?" I demanded, my voice trembling with urgency.

The nurse's expression was a mix of sympathy and professionalism, but her words hit me like a punch to the gut. "She's lost a lot of blood. She's in surgery now, but there's... there's a 30% chance she makes it."

Those words hung in the air like a death sentence, echoing in my mind as I felt my world crumble around me. I collapsed onto the floor, the cold tiles biting into my skin. My anger, my hurt, all of it felt meaningless now. *Was it worth it? All the fights, the misunderstandings, the distance between us? Would I ever get to hold her in my arms again, to feel the warmth of her smile against my cheek?*

"Who did this to her?" I asked through trembling lips, my voice barely above a whisper. Just then, Mackinzie appeared around the corner, her face bruised and battered, shades of purple and blue marring her complexion. Her lip was busted, swollen and red, and she held an ice pack against her face.

"It was Kel," she said, her voice shaky, tears welling in her eyes. "He did this to me and her."

I stood up, a surge of rage coursing through my veins. Without thinking, I punched the wall as hard as I could. Pain shot through my hand, but it was nothing compared to the rage boiling inside me. "I'll kill him!" I screamed, the sound echoing through the sterile halls. But even as the words left my mouth, a part of me felt hollow. *What good would it do?*

Mackinzie wrapped her arms around me, her body shaking as she began to cry. "Dom, please... just stop. She's in there fighting for her life."

"Natalie already did kill him," she muttered, the words laced with bitterness and helplessness.

Just then, a doctor emerged from the operating room, his face stoic, devoid of emotion. My breath hitched in my throat as I saw him holding a clipboard, my heart racing with dread.

"The surgery was a success," he said, and for a moment, hope flickered in my chest. But then his words turned cold and clinical. "However, there's something wrong with her brain. She's in a coma. This may last for hours... or even years. It's too early to tell."

The world shattered around me. I felt the air leave my lungs, a scream tearing from my throat that echoed through the sterile hospital corridors, reverberating off the walls like a haunting melody of despair. I screamed until my voice was hoarse, my body shaking with the force of my grief. Mackinzie sobbed in my arms, our tears mingling as we clung to each other, two souls lost in a sea of anguish.

At that moment, I felt utterly alone. The fear of losing Natalie consumed me, a darkness that threatened to swallow me whole. I could already envision a world without her—one devoid of laughter, of warmth, of love. I thought of all the moments we had shared: the quiet evenings spent on the couch, the way her eyes sparkled when she talked about her dreams, her laughter that filled the emptiness in my heart.

"Please, no," I whispered, my voice breaking. "Not her. She can't leave me. Not like this." The thought of her slipping away, of never seeing her smile again, twisted my insides into a painful knot.

Mackinzie's grip tightened around me, her sobs echoing in the empty hallway. "We have to stay strong for her, Dom. We can't give up hope."

But how could I hope when the very foundation of my world felt like it was crumbling? The anger I had felt earlier—anger at everything, at everyone—faded into a deep, penetrating sadness. I felt like I was standing on the edge of a precipice, staring into an abyss of uncertainty. *What if I was too late? What if I never got the chance to tell her how much I loved her, how much she meant to me?*

I closed my eyes, the tears streaming down my face as the weight of despair pressed down on me. Everything I had taken for granted, every argument we'd had, every moment I'd let slip away—I would give anything to have her back. I would trade every ounce of anger, every moment of stubborn pride, just to hold her one more time.

As time dragged on, the environment of the hospital became a blur of faces and voices. Nurses came and went, their expressions sympathetic but detached. I felt like I was watching the world from behind a glass wall, trapped in my own torment.

"Dom," Mackinzie said softly, pulling me from my thoughts. "We need to be strong for her. She's going to need us when she wakes up."

I nodded, but the doubt lingered in my heart like a

shadow. *What if she didn't wake up? What if this was it?* The thought was unbearable, a weight that pressed heavily on my chest.

I looked at Mackenzie, her face still swollen and bruised. "You need to take care of yourself too," I said, my voice strained. "You've been through so much."

"I'm fine," she insisted, but I could see the pain in her eyes, the remnants of fear lingering just beneath the surface.

We sat together in the waiting room, the sterile atmosphere filled with the sounds of muted conversations and distant beeping machines. The fluorescent lights above flickered, casting an eerie glow over everything, and I felt like I was trapped in a nightmare I couldn't wake up from.

Hours turned into what felt like days, each tick of the clock echoing the relentless passage of time. I clung to the hope that she would wake up, that I would hear her voice again, but with each passing moment, that hope felt more and more fragile.

Then, just as I thought I might lose myself completely, a nurse appeared, her expression a mix of compassion and concern. "Those waiting for Detective Fischer, you can see her now," she said softly, gesturing towards a door at the end of the hallway.

My heart raced as I stood up, Mackinzie following closely behind. We walked down the sterile corridor, the fluorescent lights buzzing overhead. Each step felt heavy, laden with the weight of uncertainty.

When we entered the room, I was struck by the sight of Natalie lying there, so still and vulnerable. She was hooked up to machines that beeped rhythmically, the steady sound a cruel reminder of the life she was fighting to maintain. Her face was pale, the bruises and cuts stark against her skin, and the sight of her like this twisted a knife in my heart.

I stepped closer, my breath hitching in my throat as I

reached for her hand, gently taking it in mine. It felt so small, so fragile. "Natalie," I whispered, my voice breaking. "It's me. I'm here. Please, please come back to me." Mackinzie stood in the corner of the room holding her arms together.

Tears streamed down my cheeks as I squeezed her hand, hoping against hope that she could feel my presence. "I love you," I said, the words pouring out of me like a desperate plea. "I need you to wake up. I can't do this without you."

Mackinzie moved to the other side of the bed, her eyes filled with tears as she reached out to brush Natalie's hair back from her forehead. "Please, Nat," she said, her voice trembling. "Fight for us. We need you."

But the silence in the room was deafening, the machines beeping a haunting reminder of the uncertainty that surrounded us. I felt like I was standing on the edge of a cliff, staring into the abyss, the fear of losing her consuming me.

"Please, Natalie," I whispered again, my voice cracking. "I can't lose you. Not now. Not ever."

The tears continued to flow, pooling in my hands as I held hers, praying for a miracle, praying for her to come back to us. The fear of losing her was a chasm I didn't know how to navigate, and in that moment, all I could do was hope against hope that she would fight her way back to us.

I must have dozed off, when the sound of relentless beeping of machines and the hushed conversations of nurses fading into a dull hum. It felt like I had only closed my eyes for a moment when the sound of a loud, screeching beep filled the room, jolting me awake. My heart raced as I saw nurses rushing into the area, their faces a mix of urgency and alarm.

"Mackinzie!" I shouted, my voice shaky as I instinctively moved to shield from the chaos. "What's happening?" She cried out as her body began to shake.

But no one answered. My mind raced, panic clawing at

my throat as I watched one of the nurses in the hallway dash towards the room, shouting "Code Blue!"

"No!" I yelled as I felt the ground beneath me shift as the words sank in. "She's flatlined."

The doctor bolted past us, an unyielding force of nature, and in that moment, I realized how helpless I truly was. "Natalie! Baby, please don't leave me!" I cried out, desperation flooding my veins.

Mackinzie slowly slid to her knees, her expression crumpling into one of utter devastation. "This is it. She's gone," she sobbed, her voice breaking as she buried her face in her hands. The sight of her anguish twisted my heart, a visceral pain that felt like a dagger to my soul.

A nurse, seemingly drawn by our despair, approached us with a hint of compassion in her eyes. "She's in surgery," she said gently, though the words felt hollow. "I promise, whenever I find out anything, I will tell you both."

Time seemed to stretch into an agonizing eternity as we sat in the waiting room, the fluorescent lights flickering above us like a cruel reminder of the reality we faced. Every second felt like an hour, the silence stretching uncomfortably between us.

Then, finally, the nurse returned, attempting to hide her relief behind a professional demeanor. "There was a blood clot, but we got it. She is stable now," she informed us. Relief washed over me, though it was tinged with a lingering fear. "They'll keep her in the ICU tonight, but tomorrow they'll move her back to a regular room. You two should go home and rest."

I looked at Mackinzie, her eyes swollen from crying and the bruises darkening on her face a stark reminder of the violence she had endured. "Come on, kid," I said softly, trying to muster a semblance of strength. "Let's get you some ice for that face and some food."

MIKEL WILSON

Mackinzie nodded, her movements slow and heavy, as if the weight of the world rested on her shoulders. We stepped outside, the cool night air hitting us like a splash of cold water. I inhaled deeply, trying to shake off the terror that clung to me like a shadow.

As we made our way to the car, the streets felt strangely alien, the lights blurring into streaks of color as I struggled to focus. The ride back home was quiet, the weight of the day settling heavily in the silence between us. The fear of losing Natalie still loomed large in my heart, but I pushed it aside, telling myself to focus on the present.

Once home, I tried to eat something—anything—but the food felt like sawdust in my mouth, tasteless and dry. I forced myself to swallow a few bites, knowing I needed to regain strength for the next day. Sleep didn't come easy, but exhaustion finally pulled me under, the memories of the day flooding my mind in a turbulent wave as I drifted into a restless slumber, my heart still tethered to the fate of the woman I loved. We made our way back to the hospital soon as the sun rose. To find Natalie in a room sleeping peacefully I sat beside her and held her hand while Mackinzie sat on the other side of her praying that she would pull through.

CHAPTER 19

NATALIE

Slowly darkness dissipated and light was allowed back into my eyes. The last thing I remember was being in the ambulance. I looked around for a minute and the first thing I felt upon waking was a disorienting heaviness, like I was swimming through molasses, each movement slow and laborious. My eyelids fluttered open, the bright fluorescent lights above casting an unforgiving glare that made me squint. It took a moment for my vision to focus, the world around me coming into view in blurry fragments. I could hear a steady beep-beep-beep rhythm in the background, a sound that felt both familiar and foreign, like an unwelcome reminder of where I was.

As the fog of unconsciousness began to lift, I realized I was lying in a hospital bed, the sterile scent of antiseptic filling my nostrils. Panic surged within me, a tidal wave of fear crashing over my senses. I tried to sit up, but a wave of dizziness washed over me, forcing me to close my eyes again. "What happened? Where am I?" I thought, my mind racing through the last few memories I could grasp.

Slowly, I turned my head, and that's when I saw them—Dom and Mackinzie, their faces etched with concern, relief, and a profound sadness that sent a chill down my spine. They were sitting side by side in the hard plastic chairs, their bodies tense, as if they had been waiting for me to wake for an eternity.

"Mackinzie?" I whispered, my voice hoarse and barely audible.

Her head snapped up, and in an instant, tears filled her eyes. "Natalie!" she cried, her voice trembling with emotion as she leaped to my side. "You're awake!"

I tried to reach for her, but my limbs felt heavy and unresponsive. "What happened?" I managed to croak, my throat dry and scratchy. "Why am I here?"

Dom leaned forward, his expression a mixture of relief and worry, his brow furrowed as if he were trying to process a whirlwind of emotions. "You've been in a coma for three days, Nat," he said softly, his voice steady but laced with an undercurrent of pain. "You were stabbed... badly."

The memories flooded back in flashes—chaos, screams, the feeling of warm blood, the sense of impending doom. I squeezed my eyes shut, the images swirling in my mind like a kaleidoscope of horror. "Mackinzie," I whispered, desperate to understand. "Are you okay? "

She shook her head vehemently, her hand squeezing mine tightly. "I'm fine, I promise! I'm okay. You're the one we were worried about. You almost didn't make it. I thought... I thought I might lose you."

The gravity of her words crashed over me, and I felt a lump form in my throat. *I had nearly died.* The thought sent a shiver coursing through my body, and I could feel the tears welling in my eyes. "What about... what about the case?" I asked, the urgency in my voice rising. "Did they catch him? Did they find any leads?"

Dom exchanged a glance with Mackinzie, and the expression on his face turned serious, somber.

"They found another victim," he said quietly, his words hanging heavily in the air. "Another one of the Crow's victims. It's been a mess, Nat. They're still investigating, but... it's bigger than we thought."

A chill ran down my spine, the implications of his words settling in like a fog. "What do you mean?" I asked, my voice trembling as I struggled to process the information. "Who else has he hurt?"

Mackinzie leaned closer, her eyes darkening with sorrow. "They found a woman in an abandoned warehouse. She was... she was in really bad shape, Natalie. The police think it's connected to you. The captain called and said as soon as you're able he needs you and Dom to come in, it's about both of your cases."

I felt my heart drop into my stomach, a wave of nausea washing over me. "Oh God," I whispered, horrified. "What happened to her?"

"They're still trying to identify her," Dom replied, his voice steady but his eyes betraying the anguish he felt. "But they think she may be the first victim. They're working round the clock to figure out how many victims there are."

I closed my eyes, the weight of the world crashing down on me. I thought of the woman—somebody's sister, daughter, friend—someone who had suffered and died. The thought was suffocating, a crushing realization that reverberated through my entire being.

Dom's hand found mine, his grip firm and reassuring.

"We're going to figure this out together. You're not alone in this, Natalie. We'll find a way to stop him."

"But what if it's too late?" I whispered, feeling the tears spill over and cascade down my cheeks. "What if I can't help? What if I'm not strong enough?"

Mackinzie wiped her own tears away, her expression fierce. "You are strong, Natalie. You're the strongest person I know. You survived this. You can't give up now. We need you."

As I looked into her eyes, I could see the fire that burned within her. It was infectious, igniting a spark in my own heart. I took a deep breath, fighting against the wave of despair that threatened to consume me. "What if I hadn't woken up? What if I had died?"

Dom's expression hardened, and he leaned closer, his voice low and serious. "You can't think like that. You're here now, and that's what matters. We'll get through this together, but you have to promise me that you'll fight. You have to fight for yourself and for the people who need you."

The room was filled with a heavy silence, the reality of our situation settling in like a dark cloud. I thought about the woman who had suffered at the hands of the Crow, about the lives that had been shattered because of his cruelty. The weight of it all felt like a lead blanket on my chest, but I wouldn't let it crush me. I would rise to the challenge. I began unplugging the stuff from my chest and I pulled out my IV

In that moment, the door creaked open, and a nurse stepped in, her presence a welcome distraction. "How are we feeling today?" she asked, her voice cheerful but professional.

ma'am we can't let you go; we need to check you over.

"And I have a serial killer to catch. Bring me the signout sheet and shut up. Dom, where are my clothes?" Yelling caused my side to hurt but with another body found we needed to find out what was going on.

"They were soaked in blood and they cut them off of you. FINE I guess we need to make a trip to the house before we go to the station."

"Do you think that's a good idea? You've been in a coma for three days."

"Three days- screw that! Let's go."

But even as I made that promise, a nagging fear lingered in the back of my mind. *What if I wasn't strong enough? What if I couldn't face the darkness that lay ahead?*

The fluorescent lights of the hospital flickered overhead as I signed my release papers, a sense of both relief and trepidation swirling within me. Dom and Mackenzie stood close by, their expressions a mix of concern and determination. My side throbbed with every movement, a constant reminder of the chaos that had unfolded, but I pushed the pain aside. I had a job to do.

Once we were outside, the cool air hit me like a splash of ice water, jolting me into the present moment. We climbed into Dom's car, the leather seats cool against my skin as I settled in. The ride back to our apartment felt like an eternity, the streets blurring past in a haze of muted colors. I stared out the window, my heart racing with a mix of fear and anger. The thought of the Crow, the monster who had done this to me and to others, hung heavily in my mind. I couldn't shake the feeling that time was running out.

As we pulled into the parking lot, I took a deep breath, steeling myself for what lay ahead. "Let's get this done," I muttered under my breath as we exited the car.

Dom and Mackenzie followed me into the apartment, the familiar surroundings offering a small comfort amidst the chaos. I glanced at Mackenzie, who looked up at me with

MIKEL WILSON

wide, worried eyes. "You can stay here, okay? We won't be gone long," I reassured her, my voice softer than I intended.

"Promise?" she asked, her voice barely above a whisper as she wrapped her arms around me, pulling me into a tight embrace.

"I promise," I said, kissing her forehead gently, feeling the warmth of her love radiate through me. It was the anchor I needed amidst the storm of emotions swirling within.

As I made my way to my room to change clothes, I could feel the weight of their gazes on me. I closed the door behind me and took a moment to gather my thoughts. The bandages on my side were a stark reminder of how close I had come to losing it all. I shook my head, frustrated at the circumstances. "Little idiot got me good," I muttered to myself, glancing at the dressing that was stained with a hint of blood.

I slid on a fresh shirt, wincing as it brushed against my injuries. Just then, Dom entered the room, his expression a mix of concern and determination. "You don't have to do this right now. You need to rest," he said, his voice firm but gentle.

"Look, I get your concern," I shot back, my voice rising with unrestrained anger. "But do you really want someone's blood on your hands? I've got enough of my own, personally." The words hung in the air between us, heavy with an unspoken truth.

"I get it," Dom replied, his voice steady, as if he understood the depths of my rage and fear.

"Let's go," I said, the urgency in my tone leaving no room for argument.

As we exited the room, Mackinzie wrapped her arms around me again, her embrace grounding me in a way nothing else could. I kissed her forehead once more, feeling the warmth of her love seep into my bones. "I'll be back soon,

I promise," I whispered, trying to infuse my words with reassurance.

"Be careful," she replied, her voice trembling slightly.

"I will," I assured her before we stepped out the door, the weight of the world resting heavily on my shoulders as we made our way to the precinct. I felt the anger simmering beneath the surface, a fire that fueled my determination to find the Crow and make him pay for the pain he had caused.

CHAPTER 20

NATALIE

The air within the precinct buzzed with urgency as we finally arrived at the station. I could feel the tension in the air, a palpable energy that buzzed around me like static electricity. Dom and I made our way down the narrow hallway, the sound of our footsteps echoing against the tiled floor. Each step felt heavier than the last as we approached Captain Howard's office, the weight of what lay ahead pressing down on me.

As I pushed the door open, I was met with Captain Howard's intense gaze. "Detective, I'm happy you're okay," he said, his voice gruff but laced with relief. "I had IA breathing down my neck to pull you off this case. But... after finding this out, I have to let you find the monster." He handed me a file, his expression serious as I took it from him.

I opened the file, and my stomach dropped. Inside were pictures of what was believed to be the Crow's first victim, the body lying on its side with a crow burned beside it. The image was grotesque, and I felt bile rise in my throat as I stared at the lifeless form.

"Okay, Captain, what does this have to do with me?" I asked, my voice trembling with a mix of dread and anger.

Captain Howard cleared his throat, rubbing the bridge of his nose as if trying to alleviate a headache. "We ran forensics on her hair and teeth, and it would seem the first victim.... is your mother."

My world tilted on its axis. The news hit me like a freight train, a wave of nausea washing over me. Finding out my mother was one of the Crow's first victims sent me spiraling. My father had always insisted she simply moved on, but the truth felt like a knife twisted in my gut. My sister was only five when she left us—to be with her boyfriend, my soccer coach. The memories flooded back, images of a young girl left behind, confused and lost.

"Nice. So she's dead. Am I supposed to feel something?" I spat, each word laced with disdain. The anger bubbled within me, directed not just at the situation but at her—my mother who had abandoned us, who had chosen a man over her own family.

"Detective, that's not—" Captain Howard began, but I cut him off.

"Thanks for the file," Dom interjected, grabbing me by the arm and leading me out of the office. "Listen, you haven't said crap to me about your mother, so I never asked. But the fact that the Crow killed her and she may be the first kill makes her my business. So let's figure this out."

I jerked my arm out of his grip, anger surging through me like a wildfire. "You don't get to decide what's my business!" I shouted, storming down the hall, my heart racing with a mix of fury and despair. I pushed through the exit doors, the cool air hitting my face like a slap. I needed to breathe, to escape the suffocating weight of the revelations swirling around me.

I sat in the car, my hands gripping the steering wheel tightly, knuckles white with tension. Dom followed behind me, opening the door and sliding into the passenger seat, his footsteps heavy as he approached. "Tell me what happened?" he begged, his voice soft but urgent.

"Fine!" I yelled, the anger spilling over. I took a deep breath, trying to rein in my emotions, but the words came tumbling out like a dam breaking. "She left us! She just walked out one day, like we didn't matter. My sister was still a baby, and I was old enough to understand what it meant to be abandoned. She chose him over us!"

The memories flooded back—my mother's laughter that faded into silence, the empty seat at the dinner table, the way my father tried to hold it all together but crumbled under the weight of her absence. "I grew up thinking she just didn't want us anymore. And now I find out she's dead? Killed by some monster? What the heck am I supposed to feel?"

Dom remained silent, giving me space to unleash the torrent of emotions that had been pent up for so long. I could see the understanding in his eyes, the empathy that made me feel both seen and vulnerable. "I can't believe she's gone," I continued, my voice thick with emotion. "I spent my whole life resenting her, and now... now I'll never get to confront her. I'll never get the answers I need."

"Nat," Dom said softly, stepping closer as I held onto the steering wheel, my body trembling with rage and sorrow. "You deserve to feel what you feel. It's okay to be angry. But we need to focus on finding this Crow. We need to make sure he pays for what he's done, not just to your mother, but to everyone."

I looked at him, the fire in my chest slowly dimming as the reality of our situation set in. "You're right," I said, my voice quieter now. "I can't let my anger consume me. Not now. Not when there are people out there who need justice."

"Exactly," Dom replied, his expression firm but supportive. "We'll find him together. We'll bring him down and make sure he pays for every life he's taken."

With a deep breath, I nodded, feeling the weight of my mother's ghost still pressing down on me, but also a newfound understanding of what really happened. I wouldn't let her choices dictate my life any longer. I would be the one to stop the pain, to seek justice for her and for all the victims of the Crow.

Dom stared at me from the passenger's seat, his expression a storm of frustration and concern. I could feel the tension radiating from him as he turned to face me, his jaw clenched tightly. "Now, you said she chose a man over you. Who was the man?" His voice was steady, but there was an edge to it, a desperate need for clarity amidst the chaos.

I exhaled deeply, the air feeling thick in my lungs. "My soccer coach—the same soccer coach I had from the time I was five. His name was Ben Sawyer." The name tasted bitter on my tongue, a reminder of the wounds that had never fully healed.

Dom's eyes widened slightly, the realization dawning on him. "Ben Sawyer? You mean the one who was… involved with her?"

"Yeah," I replied, my voice dripping with disdain. "He was more than just a coach to me; he was like an uncle type figure, and then he just… took her away." I felt the anger simmering beneath the surface, mixed with a deep-seated pain that had festered for years. "I can't believe she would choose him over her own family. It's like she didn't care about us at all."

"Fine," Dom said, his tone shifting to one of purpose. "Now we have something. We need to find Ben Sawyer and see if there's a connection. He may just be the serial killer we are looking for." As he spoke, he reached over and took my hand, squeezing it gently. It was a small gesture, but it sent a rush of warmth through me—a reminder that I wasn't alone in this fight.

"Yeah, whatever," I snapped, the frustration spilling out of me like a broken dam. The pain in my side throbbed, a constant reminder of the physical and emotional wounds I carried. "We can look for him if you want, but it'll lead us to nothing." I rolled my eyes, the movement igniting a fresh wave of discomfort that made me wince.

"Come on, Natalie," he said, his voice softer now, almost pleading. "We owe it to ourselves to explore every lead. You need to let this out. I know it hurts, but we have to do this."

I sighed, the weight of his words pressing down on me. "Fine, let's go inside and search the database," I relented, knowing that he was right, even if I was too stubborn to admit it.

We exited the car, and as we walked towards the precinct, each step felt heavy, my body protesting as I pushed through the pain. The throbbing in my side was relentless, a reminder of the violent encounter that had nearly taken my life. I could feel the anger and fear swirling within me, threatening to pull me under.

Inside the precinct, the fluorescent lights buzzed overhead, casting a harsh glare on the sterile environment. The familiar sounds of ringing phones and muffled conversations echoed around us, a constant reminder of the urgency of our work. Dom led me to a computer terminal, his expression focused as he began to type in search queries.

As I leaned against the desk, I couldn't shake the feeling of being trapped in a nightmare, the shadows of my past closing in around me. "Do you think he could be the Crow?" I asked, my voice barely above a whisper.

Dom paused, turning to look at me, his eyes filled with a combination of determination and sympathy. "It's possible.

We need to consider all the angles. If he had a connection to your mother, we can't ignore that."

I nodded, but the thought of my mother being involved with that monster filled me with a sense of dread. "I just can't believe she would... choose him. She left us. She left me. I thought she loved us," I said, my voice cracking as the hurt spilled out. I turned away, blinking back tears, feeling the anger and sorrow welling up inside me.

Dom stepped closer, his hand resting on my back, a comforting weight. "I know it's painful, Nat. But you have to confront this. You need to let it out. It's not just about the Crow; it's about finding closure for yourself. You deserve that."

I took a deep breath, his words resonating within me. "I know," I replied, my voice trembling as I fought to keep the emotions at bay. "But it's hard. It feels like a betrayal all over again. I spent my whole life resenting her for leaving, and now... now I find out she could have been a victim of this monster."

"Then let's find out the truth," Dom said, his voice firm. "We can't let her choices dictate your life any longer. We'll uncover what happened, and we'll make sure the Crow pays for what he's done."

His determination sparked something within me, a flicker of hope amidst the darkness. "You're right," I said, through gritted teeth.

CHAPTER 21

DOM

The dim glow of the computer screen illuminated my cluttered desk as I sat there, fingers poised above the keyboard, thoughts racing through my mind. The weight of the world felt heavier than ever, and my heart ached as I scrolled through the search results. I had barely begun to process the loss of my parents when the news of Natalie's mother came crashing down like a tidal wave, dragging me under.

"Soccer coach, Ben Sawyer," I typed, my heart pounding as I hoped for a lead. The clatter of keys echoed in the silence of my room, but it felt like I was typing into a void, searching for answers that wouldn't come.

Just then, Natalie's phone buzzed next to me, and I glanced at her screen. It was Mackinzie, her younger sister. My heart sank slightly, knowing what Natalie had to share. This was a conversation that would change everything.

"Hey, Mackinzie. We need to talk," Natalie said, her voice trembling.

"What is it, sis?" Mackinzie's voice came through the line, heavy with anxiety.

"They found our mother... she's dead." The words slipped out like a jagged knife, cutting through the air.

Mackinzie went completely silent. The weight of those words hung between them like a dark cloud, heavy and suffocating.

"I will be home soon, and we can talk about it," Natalie finally broke the silence, her voice strained and thick with emotion.

"Okay," Mackinzie's voice cracked, barely audible. I could sense the shock washing over her.

"You can call Dad. I'm busy, okay?" Natalie said, her tone sharper than she intended.

"Okay," Mackinzie replied, a hint of confusion in her voice.

After hanging up, Natalie let out a shuddering breath, and I felt the weight of her grief settle over us like a thick fog. "What do you remember about the day your mother left, Natalie?" I asked gently.

"I've been trying to remember more about that day," she replied, her voice tight with tension. "But all I can think about is... I can't believe she's gone."

"I know," I said softly, my heart aching for her. "But we need to figure this out. For both of our sakes."

There was a pause, the silence heavy with unspoken words. "Dom... you don't understand what it's like for your own mother to throw you away," she finally yelled, her voice cracking with emotion.

"I don't, but I do know what it's like to lose both parents," I snapped back, frustration boiling over. "Did you forget? My parents both died in that car crash last year. So don't tell me I don't know what that feels like! At least you still have your father."

The silence that followed was deafening. I could feel her hurt permeating the air, and suddenly, I regretted my words. But there was something deeper at play, a tension that had been building ever since the accident. I needed to know what she wasn't telling me.

"Natalie, I'm sorry. I didn't mean to—"

"No, you don't get it," she interrupted, her voice trembling. "I'm trying to hold myself together, but it's like… it's like I'm breaking apart. My mom was supposed to be there for me, and now she's gone. And my dad… he's just not the same anymore."

"I get that," I said, my voice softer now. "But we need to figure out what happened. Maybe the soccer coach has some answers. He was with her that day, right?"

"Yeah, he was," she said, her voice barely above a whisper. "But I don't even know where to start looking for him. It's like… everything is just a blur."

I took a deep breath, trying to steady my racing thoughts. "Let's try searching for the coach's name. Maybe he has a social media presence or something. We can reach out."

"Okay," she replied, her determination flickering back to life. "Let's do that."

I returned to the computer, the clacking of keys filling the silence between us. I typed in "soccer coach, local high school," hoping to find a lead. It would have helped if Natalie would have shared his name but it was like she refused to speak about it, but I was dealing with what I had for the time being. As I scrolled through the results, I could feel the tension in the air, a palpable reminder that we weren't just searching for answers; we were searching for closure.

"Natalie," I said suddenly, an idea striking me. "What if we look into the local news? Maybe there was a report about the accident."

"Good idea," she said, her voice gaining strength. "That might give us some clues."

As I searched the news archives, I couldn't shake the feeling that there was something Natalie wasn't telling me. It gnawed at the back of my mind, a persistent itch that wouldn't go away. I remembered the way she had hesitated whenever I mentioned her mother, the way her eyes had darkened with pain.

"Dom, I found something!" Natalie's voice broke through my thoughts, and I turned my attention back to the screen.

"What is it?" I asked, my pulse quickening.

"There's an article about my former coach right here. It would seem they left us in Oklahoma City and moved to Shawnee. He was the coach here for two years and then... nothing."

"Now we have to find nothing," I said, a sense of urgency creeping into my voice. "I'm up for a trip to Shawnee. Are you?"

"Yeah... let's go," she said, determination flickering in her eyes.

We climbed into my old sedan, its engine sputtering to life as I pulled out of the driveway. The drive to Shawnee from Oklahoma City was a blur of concrete and asphalt, the landscape shifting from urban sprawl to open fields dotted with trees. I could feel the tension radiating from Natalie as we drove, her silence louder than any words could be.

"Natalie, are you okay?" I asked, glancing over at her. She was staring out the window, her fingers nervously tapping against her thigh.

"I just... I don't know what to expect," she admitted, her

voice barely above a whisper. "What if we find him and he doesn't have any answers? What if it just makes everything worse?"

I reached over, placing my hand on hers for comfort. "We won't know until we try. You deserve answers, Natalie. You deserve to know what happened."

She nodded, but I could see the uncertainty etched on her face. "It's just hard, Dom. Really hard. I thought I could handle this, but now that it's real… it feels like I'm losing my grip."

I tightened my grip on the steering wheel, my heart aching for her. "You're not alone in this. I'm here, okay? We'll face whatever comes together."

The miles slipped by, and the landscape began to change as we neared Shawnee. The vibrant greens of the fields gave way to clusters of houses and small businesses, a stark reminder that life continued on, even as we were left grappling with loss.

"Natalie," I ventured again, "do you think there's something you're not telling me about your mom? Something that could help us understand why she was with Coach Sawyer?"

Her eyes flickered with hesitation. "I don't know, Dom. There are things I don't want to believe. I don't want to think she could have left us willingly. I don't want to believe she was unhappy."

"But what if she was?" I pressed gently. "What if there's more to the story? You deserve to know the truth, even if it hurts."

She drew in a shaky breath, the fight in her eyes wavering. "I just don't know if I'm ready for that truth."

We pulled into Shawnee, the streets dead without life. I parked the car outside a small diner, the neon sign flickering above us. "Let's start here," I suggested. "If anyone knows Coach Sawyer, it's probably someone in this town."

As we stepped into the diner, the aroma of fried food and coffee enveloped us. The chatter of patrons filled the air, but I could feel the weight of our mission pressing down on us. We found a booth in the corner, and I could see Natalie's hands tremble slightly as she fidgeted with the menu.

"Are you hungry?" I asked, trying to lighten the mood.

"Not really," she admitted, her eyes scanning the room. "I just want to find him."

"Alright," I said, signaling the waitress for coffee. "Let's focus on that. Do you want to start by asking around?"

Natalie nodded, but I could see the fear in her eyes. "What if he doesn't want to talk to us? What if we're intruding?"

"Then we'll respect that," I said firmly. "But we owe it to your mom to at least try. We can't keep running from the truth."

After finishing our coffee, we approached an older man sitting at the counter, his weathered face telling stories of its own. "Excuse me, sir," I said, trying to keep my voice steady. "Do you happen to know Coach Sawyer?"

He looked up, squinting at us. "Sawyer? Yeah, I know him. He used to coach the high school soccer team here. Why? What do you want with him?"

Natalie stepped forward, her voice shaking. "We're looking for answers about my mom... Amy Fischer. She was with him the day she died."

"Well I don't remember a woman being with him when he was here." I'm sorry about your mother, Miss." The man looked sympathetic but unsure of how he could possibly help.

He hesitated, glancing around as if weighing his words. "Last I heard, he moved out of state.

"Do you know of any way we could find what state he moved to? Or why did he leave? " I pressed.

"I don't know anything sir. I sure hope you guys find something."

Something tells me he was hiding something but I decided not to push. The fact that Natalie's mom wasn't with him when he moved was troubling. What exactly did he do?

CHAPTER 22

DOM

The glow of the computer screen illuminated my face as I leaned back in my chair, frustration coursing through me. I had scoured every online resource I could think of, but every lead on Ben Sawyer, the soccer coach who had vanished after the accident, had led to a dead end. "It's like he disappeared into thin air," I muttered to myself. I glanced over at Natalie, who sat across from me, her expression a mix of determination and despair.

"Dom, I just don't understand how someone can just go missing like this," she said, her voice cracking. "He was there that day… he must know something."

"I know," I replied, my fingers flying over the keyboard as I searched social media, hoping to find a trace of him. Facebook, Twitter, Instagram—nothing. It was as if he had been erased from existence. "No posts, no updates. It's like he's a ghost."

Natalie ran her fingers through her hair, her eyes glistening with unshed tears. "If he's the one who knows what happened to my mom… if he has answers… then why isn't he talking? Why would he just vanish?"

"It doesn't make sense," I admitted, frustration bubbling beneath my skin. "But we need to keep looking. If he's connected to your mom's death, we have to find him."

As we continued our search, the weight of the situation pressed heavily on us. I could feel the tension in the air, the fear of not knowing, and the uncertainty gnawing at our resolve. "What if he is involved in something more sinister?" I asked suddenly. "What if he's the Crow?"

Natalie's eyes widened, and I could see the fear creeping in. "The Crow? You think he's a serial killer?"

"I don't know, but there's something off about this whole situation. We know he was with your mom, and now he's missing. It's the perfect setup."

The thought hung in the air between us, heavy and unsettling. We had been chasing the truth, but what if the truth was darker than we ever imagined?

After hours of searching between the database of other departments, we finally hit a wall. "There's nothing," I said, my voice filled with frustration. "No leads, no connections. It's like Ben Sawyer just… doesn't exist anymore."

Natalie leaned back in her chair, her face pale. "What do we do now?"

"I wish I knew," I replied, my heart aching for her. "But maybe we should take a break, clear our heads. You could call Mackinzie?"

Natalie nodded, but I could see the hesitation in her eyes. "What do I even say to her? 'Hey, your Mother's gone, but we're still looking for answers?'"

"Just be honest. She needs to know what's going on, even if it's hard," I urged gently.

Reluctantly, Natalie picked up her phone and dialed. The ringing filled the room, each tone echoing our anxiety. When Mackinzie finally answered, the tension in Natalie's voice was palpable.

"Hey, Mackinzie," Natalie said, her voice trembling.

"Nat? What's wrong?" Mackinzie's voice was laced with concern, and I could hear the tremor in her tone.

"Nobody knows where Coach Sawyer is. We've been searching for hours, but it's like he just vanished... and I don't know what to do."

"Is he... is he the one who hurt Mom?" Mackinzie asked, her voice breaking.

"I don't know," Natalie admitted, tears pooling in her eyes. "But we're not giving up. I promise you that. We just need to keep looking."

I could hear the quiet sobs from Mackinzie's end of the line, and it shattered my heart. "I'm scared, Nat. What if we can't find him? What if no one knows what really happened?"

"We will find him, Mackinzie. We have to believe that," Natalie said, her voice steadier now, though I could hear the cracks of her own fear beneath the surface.

"I don't want to lose you too," Mackinzie whispered, the vulnerability in her voice hitting me like a wave.

"You won't lose me. I'm right here," Natalie reassured her, her voice softening. "We're in this together, okay? I won't let anything happen to you."

"Okay," Mackinzie said, her voice still shaky. "But I wish Dad would just tell us what he knows. Why can't he just talk to us?"

"That's something I don't understand either," Natalie replied, frustration creeping back into her tone. "He's acting like everything is normal, like we can just pretend none of this happened."

As Natalie and Mackinzie continued their conversation, I

could see the emotional toll it was taking on both of them. The weight of their mother's loss hung heavy in the air, and the uncertainty about what had happened only amplified their grief.

"Mackinzie, I know this is hard, but we need to stay strong," Natalie said, her voice firm. "We need to keep asking questions, even if it hurts."

"I just don't want to feel like a burden," Mackinzie admitted, her voice barely above a whisper.

"You're not a burden," Natalie insisted, her eyes glistening with tears. "You're my sister, and I love you. We'll get through this together."

After hanging up, Natalie wiped her eyes and took a deep breath. "I feel like I'm falling apart, Dom. I don't know how much longer I can keep this up."

"You're not alone, Natalie. I'm here for you, no matter what," I said, trying to offer her some comfort.

"Thanks, Dom. I just... I wish I could take all this pain away from Mackinzie. She shouldn't have to deal with this," she said, her voice trembling.

As we sat in silence, the weight of our search pressing down on us, I couldn't shake the feeling that we were running out of time. "Maybe we should head back home," I suggested, my mind racing. "If Natalie's mom was found here, there has to be some clue or something we're missing."

"Yeah," she said with a sigh. "Maybe I should have started there."

The drive back felt longer than it should have. The air in the car was thick with unspoken words, the weight of our emotions hanging heavily between us. I could see Natalie's face reflected in the rearview mirror, a mixture of determination and despair etched into her features.

"Do you think Dad is hiding something?" she asked suddenly, breaking the silence.

"I don't know," I replied cautiously. "But it feels like he's not being honest with you or Mackinzie. He should be talking to you about this."

Natalie nodded. "He wants to give Mom a funeral even after everything. I don't understand how he can do that. She left us. She left him."

I could hear the pain in her voice, the confusion and anger swirling together. "It's complicated," I said gently. "Grief makes people act in ways you wouldn't expect. Maybe he's trying to find closure for himself, even if it's not what you want."

"But what about us?" she cried, her voice rising in frustration. "What about the closure we need? He can't just pretend everything is okay!"

"I know," I said softly. "But maybe he's just trying to protect you both from the pain of it all. It's hard for him too."

"Or maybe he's just burying his head in the sand," she shot back, her voice filled with frustration. "I can't believe he wants to give her a funeral when she didn't even care enough to stay with us!"

"Natalie, it's okay to be angry," I said, my heart aching for her. "You have every right to feel that way. But remember, he's still your father. This is hard for him too."

"Maybe," she replied, her voice quieter now. "But I just wish he would talk to us. I wish he would let us in."

As we continued driving, I could see the landscape shifting, the familiar roads of home drawing closer. But the sense of dread loomed over us, like a storm cloud waiting to burst.

When we finally arrived back at home,the weight of everything settled over us. The house felt empty, devoid of the warmth and love that had once filled it. When Mackinzie came in from outside carrying a dog.

"Uuum, Mackinzie, where'd the dog come from?"

Mackinzie looked like she had seen a ghost when she held

him close to her chest. The gray chunky dog was smiling while she rubbed its back.

"And just where has it been staying?" Mackinzie's eyes slowly looked over towards the floor where there was a doggy bed and nice little stains all over the carpet.

"First you bought a dog and then you brought it to the house so it could leave little treats on our carpet?" Natalie asked, her nose flared.

"First of all he's a bully breed, and second his name is Stitch, and third, you killed my boyfriend! The least you could do is be a little nicer to me."

"He was beating you like a pinata. Maybe a 'thank you' wouldn't be out of the question."

"Okay both of you to your corners. I swear. Between this case, you almost dying, you getting beat up, and us finding nothing on the trip, I am exhausted! Can we please have a quiet evening?!" I yelled, pointing my fingers in both directions.

"I'm sorry." they both said in unison before they hugged. Now that's better, I said , shaking my head.

She put the puppy on the floor and he hunkered down and started barking at me. Okay, okay- my heart melted for a minute. "Come here, little guy. Well look at him! Natalie, he's so cute." I sat on the floor and began to play with Stitch when Mackinzie folded her arms and sarcastically said, "Told ya so."

"Okay, okay," Natalie laughed. "He can stay. But you better get him away from Dom-he may steal him." I chuckled also, relieved that some of the tension in the room had been released.

The night went by well. I played with Stitch and we had takeout Chinese food and watched a movie before bed. Natalie was exhausted as she fell asleep halfway through the movie. I lifted her up and put her in bed. I then came back to the living room and rubbed Stitch's head before kissing Mackinzies forehead. "Get some sleep dork." I chuckled before she wrapped her arms around me and hugged me. *She had been through so much but still had an innocence about her. She was special just like her big sister.*

CHAPTER 23

NATALIE

After getting breakfast with Dom I walked into my living room where I was shocked to see my father was sitting, his face buried in a newspaper. He looked up, surprise flickering across his features. It had been awhile since he had seen me wearing my natural hair color. Usually I kept it blonde. Mackinzie was sitting beside him with a big smile on her face while Stitch drugged one of my pillows across the floor. When I stood there with my arms folded everything went silent and stitch stopped moving pretending like he wasn't just tearing up one of my pillows.

"Natalie?" he said, his voice trembling.

"Dad, nice to see Mackinzie invited you to my house, because we need to talk," I said. I tried to stay calm and steady despite the tremor in my hands.

"About what?" he asked, shifting uncomfortably in his seat.

"About Mom," I yelled, the words falling heavy between us. "We need answers, and you're not giving them to us."

He sighed, running a hand through his hair. "I know this is hard, but I'm doing what I think is best for our family."

"Best for our family?" I echoed, disbelief flooding her voice. "You want to give her a funeral? After everything she did? She left us, Dad!"

"I know she did," he said, his voice strained. "But she was still your mother. You have to understand that."

"Understand what?" I shot back, anger rising in her chest. "That she abandoned us? That she chose to leave us behind?"

"Maybe she didn't choose it, Natalie. Maybe there were things you don't understand," he replied, frustration creeping into his voice. "I loved her once. I still do, in a way. I can't just erase that."

"Love?" I scoffed, tears streaming down her face. "How can you love someone who hurt us so deeply? She left you, she left us. That's not love, Dad. That's betrayal!"

"I'm not asking you to forgive her," he said, his voice rising. "But I want to give her a proper send-off. It's what I believe she deserves."

"What she deserves?" I could feel my voice tremble with emotion. "What about what we deserve? We deserve the truth, Dad! We deserve to know why she left and what really happened!"

My father's face fell, the weight of her words crashing over him. "I just don't want to believe the worst," he said quietly, his voice breaking. "I can't. Not yet."

"But we need to," I insisted, my voice steady. "We need to know the truth so we can move on. I can't keep living in this limbo, wondering why she left, or worse... why she had to die."

There was a long silence, the tension thick in the air.

Finally, their father spoke, his voice barely above a whisper. "I'll help you find the answers, Natalie. I promise. But it's going to hurt."

My father cleared his throat, the sound heavy and thick as he leaned back in his chair, exhaling slowly, the weight of unspoken truths hanging heavy in the air. "I wasn't a good man, Natalie," he began, his voice sincere but laced with regret.

"Your mother hid my issues... my issues with alcohol, and I was abusive."

He clasped his hands together, looking down at his lap, as if the fabric of his jeans held the answers to our family's pain. I could see Mackinzie's face twist in horror, her eyes wide as she stared at him, unable to comprehend the revelation. *I had only vague memories of his drinking and the fights that erupted like thunderstorms in the night. I never knew he had been abusive.*

"If you want to know why your mother left, a lot of it had to do with what I did," he continued, his voice trembling. "If you want someone to blame for her leaving, blame me."

The room felt like it was closing in on us, the air thick with tension. "What do you mean?" I asked, my voice a tight whisper, a mix of anger and disbelief swirling inside me.

He took a deep breath, his eyes glistening with unshed tears. "One day, I got drunk. I caught her trying to leave with you girls, and I smacked her. I grabbed her and made her a promise—if she took my daughters away, I would find her and kill her."

The confession hung in the air, a heavy stone sinking to the bottom of my stomach. "So you killed Mom? Is that a confession?" I asked, my voice rising, the disbelief turning into a volcanic anger.

"So she left with Coach because you pushed her to leave us?"

"So all these years, you let us believe she left us? That we weren't good enough? You are the reason? The reason I didn't have my mom there for prom? To hold my hand through all of my firsts?"

I could feel the heat radiating off me, the fury boiling over. "You are a sad excuse of a man and a coward!"

"Dom," he pleaded, glancing at me as if he were the anchor in this storm. "You need to breathe."

I jerked my hand away from him, unable to stand his touch. "Don't. Just don't," I said, my voice sharp as I walked closer to him, the space between us crackling with unsaid emotions. I could see the pain etched on his face, but it only fueled my anger.

Mackinzie had gotten up from her seat, her arms folded tightly across her chest, a mirror of the conflict I felt inside. "How could you tell us you're the reason we lost our mother?" she asked, her voice barely above a whisper. "How could you do this to us?"

"I don't expect you girls to forgive me," he said, his voice breaking, the weight of his confession crashing over him like waves. "But how could I not tell you? I was terrified of what you would think of me."

Tears streamed down his face, and I could see the regret etched into every line of his expression. "I went and got help for my drinking and tried to be the best dad I could be," he said, his voice a raw whisper.

"But you weren't our mother!" Mackinzie cried out, her voice filled with anguish. The words struck like a dagger, and I could see the pain in her eyes as she looked at him.

"Girls, at least you have a dad still," Dom said, his voice calm but firm. "He made mistakes. We're all human; we all do. But he's trying to make things right. Maybe you three should go talk."

"Talk?" I scoffed, the anger boiling inside me. "I don't even want to look at him." I turned on my heel and stormed down the hall, slamming the door to my room behind me. The sound echoed in the silence, a finality that reverberated through the house.

Inside my room, I leaned against the door, my heart racing. I felt the warmth of tears spilling down my cheeks, each drop a mix of anger, sadness, and confusion. *How could he have kept this from us for so long? How could he think that this was something we could just forgive?* The betrayal cut deeper than I had ever imagined.

Moments later, I heard a soft knock on my door. "Nat?" It was Dom's voice, gentle and reassuring. "Can I come in?"

I wiped my tears away with the back of my hand, trying to compose myself. "Yeah," I said, my voice muffled.

He opened the door, stepping inside and closing it behind him. "You okay?" he asked, concern etched on his face.

"No!" I cried out, my voice cracking. "I'm not okay! How could he do that to us, Dom? How could he let us believe that we weren't worth staying for?"

"I don't know, Natalie," he said, his voice softening as he sat on the edge of my bed. "But what he did was wrong. It's not your fault. You didn't ask for any of this."

"But he's still our dad," I said, the conflict raging inside me. "I should feel something for him. I should want to forgive him. But I can't. Not after what he just told us."

"Maybe it's too soon," he said, his voice steady. "You're allowed to feel angry. You're allowed to feel hurt. This is a huge revelation, and it changes everything. But it doesn't mean you have to forgive him today or tomorrow. Take your time."

I nodded, the truth of his words washing over me like a balm. "It just hurts so much," I admitted, my voice trembling. "I thought I could handle it, but now... I feel like my whole life has been a lie."

"Sometimes the truth is harder to bear than the lie," he

said softly. "But you're stronger than you think. You've made it this far, and you'll keep going. Just give yourself some grace."

"I don't even know where to start," I said, my heart heavy. "Everything feels so broken."

"Start by allowing yourself to feel," he replied, his eyes steady on mine. "You don't have to figure everything out right now. Just take it one step at a time."

I took a deep breath, trying to steady my racing heart. "Do you really think he wants to change? Do you think he's sincere?"

"I think he's trying to make amends in his own way," Dom said, his voice thoughtful. "But it's going to take time for him to prove that to you. And it's going to take time for you to trust him again."

Just then, I heard a soft knock on the door again, and my heart sank. "Can we talk?" It was Mackinzie.

"Yeah, come in," I said, my voice filled with a mix of anxiety and anticipation.

Mackinzie stepped inside, her face still pale, her eyes red from crying. "Nat, I... I don't know what to say," she said, her voice shaky. "I just can't believe what we heard."

"I know," I replied, my heart aching for her. "What he said... it changes everything."

"Do you think we can ever forgive him?" Mackinzie asked, her voice trembling. "How can we trust him after this?"

"I don't know," I admitted, my heart heavy with uncertainty. "But we need to take it one day at a time. I'm not ready to forgive him, and I don't know if I ever will be. But we need to be honest with ourselves and each other."

Mackinzie nodded, her expression thoughtful. "I just wish things were different. I wish Mom was here." A knock

MIKEL WILSON

at the door interrupted our conversation. "Hello girls. Please, just come out and talk to me."

"Fine, we will be out in a minute." I snapped.

After a long conversation filled with tears and uncertainty, Mackinzie and I exchanged a determined glance. "Okay," I said softly, my voice steadying. "Let's go talk to him."

We walked back into the living room, the atmosphere heavy with unspoken words. My father sat on the couch, his hands clasped tightly together, his face a mixture of anxiety and regret. As we stepped in, he looked up, his eyes widening with hope and fear.

"Girls," he said, his voice trembling. "I—"

Before he could finish, he dropped to his knees in front of us, the movement startling both of us. "Please, forgive me," he begged, his voice cracking. "I know I've hurt you both in ways I can't even begin to express. I've been a terrible father, and I've let my demons destroy our family. But I'm begging you, please give me a chance to make things right."

Mackinzie's eyes widened in shock, and I felt a rush of emotions swirl within me—anger, pity, and an unexpected tenderness. "Dad, getting on your knees isn't going to change what you did," I said, my voice barely above a whisper.

"I know that," he replied, tears streaming down his cheeks. "But I need you to know how deeply sorry I am. I'm sorry for the pain I caused your mother, for the fear I put in her heart, and for all the times I let you down. I can't take back the past, but I want to be better. I want to be the father you deserve."

"Then why didn't you just tell us?" Mackinzie asked, her voice shaking. "All those years, why did you let us believe Mom left because of us?"

"Because I was scared," he admitted, his voice thick with emotion. "I didn't know how to face the truth. I thought if I kept my mouth shut, it would protect you both from the reality of what happened. But I see now that it only hurt you more. I was a coward, and I'm so sorry."

I could see the sincerity in his eyes, the guilt and regret that weighed heavily on his shoulders. "We've spent so much time feeling abandoned, Dad," I said, my voice breaking. "You were supposed to be our protector, and instead, you were part of the problem."

"I know," he said, his voice trembling. "I can't change the past, but I want to change the future. I want to be there for you both, to support you and love you the way you deserve. I'm committed to getting help and being the dad you always needed."

Mackinzie stepped forward, her expression softening as she looked at him kneeling on the floor. "It's just... it's hard to trust you again," she admitted, her voice wavering. "How do we know you won't just go back to the way you were?"

"I promise you, I'm working on it," he said earnestly, his hands shaking. "I've started going to meetings, and I've been talking to a therapist. I want to be a better person for you both. I want to earn your trust back."

I exchanged a glance with Mackinzie, uncertainty still flickering in her eyes. "I want to try," I said slowly, feeling the weight of the moment pressing on my chest. "But it's going to take time. You need to understand that."

"I understand," he said, relief flooding his features. "I don't expect you to forgive me right away. I just hope you'll allow me the chance to show you I can change."

Mackinzie took a deep breath, her eyes glistening with unshed tears. "I want to believe you, Dad. I really do," she said, her voice trembling. "But it's going to be hard."

"I'm ready for hard," he said, his sincerity shining through the pain. "I'll do whatever it takes to make it right. I love you both more than I can express, and I've been a fool for taking that love for granted."

At that moment, something shifted in the air between us. I could see the vulnerability in my father's eyes, the raw honesty in his admission. Maybe it wouldn't be easy, but perhaps there was a path forward.

"Okay," I said softly, stepping closer. "Let's try. We'll try together."

Mackinzie nodded, and I could see the resolve building in her. "We can try," she echoed, her voice steadier now.

My father looked up at us, his expression a mixture of gratitude and hope. "Thank you," he whispered, his voice breaking. "Thank you for giving me a chance."

Without thinking, I stepped forward and wrapped my arms around him, pulling him into a tight embrace. It was a moment filled with uncertainty, but also a flicker of hope. "We'll figure this out, Dad," I whispered.

Mackinzie joined us, her arms wrapping around both of us, and for the first time in a long time, I felt a semblance of unity. We stood there, embracing, the weight of the past still lingering but softened by the possibility of a new beginning.

"Together," I said softly, my heart swelling with a mix of emotions. "We're in this together."

"Together," Mackinzie echoed, her voice muffled against my shoulder.

And in that moment, surrounded by the warmth of our embrace, I realized that perhaps forgiveness didn't mean forgetting; it meant choosing to move forward, one step at a time.

"We will have a funeral for mom; it's the right thing to do." I said while wiping my eyes.

"Maybe in the morning, I can take my girls out for some breakfast. Is that okay, Dom, if I steal your girlfriend away

FLAMES OF THE CROWS BETRAYAL

for a while?" Their poor dad looked sheepish and hopeful as he asked this.

"Not at all. You all need that." I said with a smile.

That night Natalie laid on my chest while I rubbed my hand through her red hair. She took a deep breath while she squeezed me. I kissed her forehead and just watched her sleep until I soon dozed off.

CHAPTER 24

DOM

*T*he girls and their dad left before I even got up. I lay in bed, staring at the ceiling, the weight of the revelations from the night before pressing heavily on my chest. My mind raced with thoughts, each one darker than the last. *Where is the one place a person can disappear, even if they don't want to? Jail. That would be a good reason why the guy acted so weird when we asked about him. What secrets was everyone hiding?*

I swung my legs over the side of the bed, the cool floor grounding me. I had to find out more about Ben Sawyer, Natalie's former soccer coach. My heart raced as I powered on my laptop, fingers trembling slightly as I typed his name into the search bar. The results popped up quickly, but it was the first link that sent a chill down my spine: "Former Soccer Coach Sentenced for Indecent Contact with Minors."

I clicked on the article, my stomach churning as I read through the details. Ben Sawyer had been in jail for years.

The charges were horrific, and as I absorbed the information, I felt a knot form in my throat. *How could someone who had been a part of Natalie's life turn out to be this monster?*

I needed to confront him. I had to know what he knew about Natalie's mother and why everyone acted so strange when we asked about him. I grabbed my keys and headed out, determination fueling my every step. I made my way to the prison he had never left. He had been here under our nose the entire time, nothing in us thought to look at the prison registry. I took the 45 minute drive to the prison.

The prison was cold and unwelcoming, the walls lined with gray concrete that seemed to absorb any light trying to escape. As I walked through the security checkpoint, my heart pounded in my chest. I had never been inside a prison before always being just a beat cop. I only took captives to the county jail. But this was another monster entirely, and the atmosphere was suffocating. The guards glanced at me with a mixture of curiosity and suspicion, but I held my head high, my purpose clear.

After what felt like an eternity, I was finally led to a small, sterile room with a table and two chairs. A guardsman stepped out first, his expression serious. "You'll have fifteen minutes. No more. You understand?"

I nodded, my stomach twisting in knots. This was it. I was about to face Ben Sawyer.

A moment later, he was brought in, chains clanking as he shuffled into the room. He looked older than I expected, his hair graying and his skin pale. But there was something in his eyes—a flicker of recognition and something darker, something that sent a shiver down my spine.

"Who are you?" he asked, his voice gravelly, almost resentful.

"I'm Dom," I said, taking a deep breath. "I'm here to talk about Amanda Fischer."

His expression shifted, the flicker of recognition morphing into something more guarded. "What do you want with her?"

"I want to know what happened to her," I replied, leaning forward. "You were with her the day she died. You were the last person to see her."

He leaned back in his chair, a smirk creeping onto his face. "Why would I know anything? I was just a coach."

"Don't play games with me, Sawyer. I know you've been in jail for years. You were a coach, but you were also a criminal," I shot back, my anger flaring. "You were accused of molestation. That's not just something you can brush aside."

He narrowed his eyes, his demeanor shifting. "You think you know everything, don't you? You think you can just waltz in here and demand answers? You have no idea what I've been through."

"Then enlighten me," I challenged, leaning closer. "Because right now, all I see is a coward who hurt innocent kids and is now hiding behind bars."

His expression darkened, the smirk fading. "You want to know about Amanda? You should ask more about her daughter Natalie ya know—she wasn't innocent either."

"What do you mean?" I asked, my heart racing, curiosity suddenly mingling with fear.

"She has secrets. She was the perfect little princess " he said, leaning forward, his eyes gleaming with a twisted satisfaction. "How is she?"

I felt my stomach drop. "What things? What are you talking about?"

"I'm in here for life; I mean, there is nothing else they can do to me. Natalie was one of my favorites and always has been. My little student."

FLAMES OF THE CROWS BETRAYAL

"Why should I believe you?" I shot back, my heart pounding. "You're a criminal. You're just trying to shift the blame."

He chuckled, a harsh, dry sound. "Maybe. But you're not ready to hear the truth. You think you're protecting her, but you're just living in a fantasy."

"What did you do to her?" I demanded, my fists clenched. "What did you do to Natalie?"

He leaned back, his expression smug. "You really want to know? You should ask her. She's the one who knows the most about our little secret."

"What little secret?" I pressed, my voice urgent.

He paused, a glint of mischief in his eyes, and I felt a chill creep down my spine.

"Stop avoiding the question!" I shouted, frustration boiling over. "What are you saying?"

He took a deep breath, his smile fading slightly. "I'm saying that if you really want to understand what happened, you need to look deeper. Natalie knows what happened. It isn't for me to say. I can see she's with you now, maybe she needs to tell you the truth. My heart raced as I processed his words. "You're lying. You're just trying to get into my head."

"Am I?" he shot back, his demeanor shifting to something darker. "You think you're the hero in this story, but there are no heroes here. Just people trying to survive."

"Survive what?" I asked, fear creeping into my voice.

"Things you can't even begin to imagine. If you're looking for answers, you need to be ready to face the truth," he said, his eyes narrowing. "And that truth might be more than you can handle."

I stood up, anger boiling over. "You're a monster, and you think you can just deflect responsibility? You think you can scare me?"

He leaned forward, his voice low and menacing. "I'm not trying to scare you, Dom. I'm trying to warn you. There are

MIKEL WILSON

forces at play that you don't understand, and if you keep digging, you might find yourself in a grave you can't climb out of."

"Then I'll take my chances," I said, my voice steady despite the fear coursing through me. "Because I'm not stopping until I find out the truth—about Natalie."

Sawyer chuckled, a dark, cynical sound. "Good luck with that. But remember, the truth never sets anyone free. It only chains you to a new reality."

As the guard entered the room to escort him away, I felt a mix of anger and dread wash over me. I had come seeking answers but left with more questions, the weight of Sawyer's words pressing heavily on my mind.

Once outside the prison walls, the air felt different—charged with tension and uncertainty. I leaned against my car, trying to process everything I had just learned. *What secrets did Natalie hold? And how deep did the rabbit hole go?*

I fished out my phone and dialed Natalie's number, my heart racing as the line rang. She answered on the third ring, her voice a mix of concern and curiosity.

"Dom? What's going on? Did you find him?"

"Yes, I did," I said, my voice steady but filled with urgency. "We need to talk. It's about your mom."

"What do you mean? What happened?" she asked, her tone shifting to one of alarm.

"Can we meet somewhere? There's a lot to discuss," I replied, my mind racing.

"Sure, where?" she asked, worry creeping into her voice.

"The park by our apartment. I'll be there in ten minutes," I said, hanging up before she could respond. I needed her to know the truth, especially if there were dangers lurking in the shadows, waiting to strike.

As I drove, I felt the weight of Sawyer's words pressing

down on me. I had to protect Natalie—whatever dark secrets her mother had hidden, whatever dangers we were about to face, I wouldn't let anything happen to her. Not now. Not ever.

The park came into view, and my heart raced as I pulled into a parking space. I could see Natalie waiting near the swings, her expression a mixture of concern and anticipation. I stepped out of the car and rushed toward her, determination fueling my every step.

"Dom, what did he say?" she asked, her eyes wide with worry.

"We need to talk," I replied, my voice urgent. "And you need to be prepared for what you're about to hear."

The sun hung low in the sky, casting a golden hue over the park, her red hair flying wildly in the wind. The rustling leaves whispered secrets, and the faint chirping of birds felt like a distant echo of normalcy. But as I made my way towards her, my heart raced, each thump matching the urgency of the moment. She looked beautiful but anxious, her brow furrowed in worry.

"Natalie," I called, waving her over, the cool air swirling around me. But as she approached, I could see the hesitation in her steps, the way her eyes flickered away from mine.

"I found Sawyer," I said, my voice steady despite the nervous energy coursing through me. "He said he knows nothing about what happened to your mother, but he had a lot to say about you."

Her expression shifted, a flicker of confusion crossing her face. "Like what?" she asked, her voice strained. "He was my soccer coach. We never really talked. I mean, I was a kid," she chuckled, but it sounded hollow, a façade that crumbled under the weight of my gaze.

"Is there anything you want to tell me?" I pressed, my

heart pounding in my chest. "Like, how long was he your coach?"

"Since I was five. Why?" she replied, defensive.

"H-he's in prison for indecent touching of a child," I stammered, watching as her face instantly changed, the color draining from her cheeks, leaving her emotionless.

"Good," she said, her voice cold and distant. "He deserves to be there if he did that."

"Baby, talk to me," I urged, stepping closer, my hand reaching out to touch hers. "Why do you think I brought you here? So we could be alone. There is nothing you can't tell me."

But when my fingers brushed against her skin, she pulled back, a wall of denial rising between us. "You don't believe me? I told you nothing happened! Why are you interrogating me? Good lord, this is ridiculous."

"No this is sad, we have a serial killer on the loose and you want to go digging into my past! Why because I didn't answer your little proposal? Is that it?"

That stung, but I knew what she was doing deflecting.

"You are in denial, Natalie," I said, my voice firm, though worry gnawed at my insides. "I have studied human behavior, like you have. Just give me your phone."

"Why? Do you need to see if I've been secretly talking to my prison boyfriend?" she snapped, her eyes flashing with anger.

"No, I'm calling your therapist. Maybe she can get through to you," I replied, my heart racing as fear coursed through my veins.

"Fine, here," she said, shoving the phone into my hands with an edge of frustration. "Call her."

I opened her phone and began scrolling for her therapist's name, the gravity of the situation weighing heavily on my shoulders. The park around us seemed to shrink, the laughter of children playing on the swings fading into an ominous silence. Just as I was about to hit the call button, the world suddenly shifted.

A sharp pain exploded in the back of my head, and everything went black.

The darkness enveloped me, thick and suffocating. I felt disoriented, my senses numbed as I tried to grasp the reality of what had just happened. My heart raced, pounding against my ribcage like a frantic drum. I was aware of the cool ground beneath me, the rough texture of grass scraping against my skin.

CHAPTER 25

DOM

I woke up with a jolt, my heart racing as I came to terms with my surroundings. The air was heavy with the smell of hay and the musty scent of old wood. Confusion swirled in my mind like a fog, thick and disorienting. I blinked several times, trying to shake off the grogginess, but as my vision cleared, panic set in. I was tied up, my wrists bound tightly with coarse rope, the fibers digging into my skin.

The dim light filtering through the gaps in the barn walls illuminated my prison, casting long shadows that danced ominously around me. I strained against the ropes, but they held firm, unyielding. My heart pounded in my chest, each beat a reminder of the fear coursing through my veins. Where was I? Where was Natalie?

I took a deep breath, trying to steady myself, but the air felt thick and stale, making my head spin. Dizziness washed over me, and I leaned back against the rough wooden wall for support. My mind raced as I struggled to piece together the events that had led me here.

The last thing I remembered was being in the park with Natalie, the tension between us palpable as we confronted the dark truths of her past. The sudden blow to my head had knocked me out cold, and now I was here, trapped in a barn, with no idea of how much time had passed.

Desperation clawed at me as I scanned the dimly lit space. The barn was old, with wooden beams creaking under the weight of time. Shadows flickered in the corners, and the distant sound of animals stirred somewhere beyond the walls. I could hear the soft rustling of hay and the occasional scuffle of feet, but there was no sign of anyone else. Just me, tied up and vulnerable.

What if I was too late? What if something had happened to Natalie? My mind raced with frantic thoughts—*had the Crow found her? Had he been watching us all along?* The realization sent a chill down my spine. The Crow wasn't just a figment of my imagination; he was real, and he was out there, lurking in the shadows.

I tried to calm my breathing, but the fear surged again. I had let my guard down. I had let my desire to protect Natalie blind me to the dangers around us. The Crow had been watching us, waiting for the right moment to strike. What had I done?

I pulled at the ropes, desperation fueling my actions. I couldn't stay here; I had to escape. I couldn't let anything happen to Natalie. The thought of her in danger sent a wave of adrenaline coursing through my body. I had to find a way out.

I twisted my wrists, trying to loosen the knots, but the ropes were too tight, cutting into my skin. Panic threatened to overwhelm me again, but I forced myself to focus. I couldn't give up. I had to think.

MIKEL WILSON

My head pounded like a drum, a relentless throb that made it hard to think clearly. Each heartbeat reverberated in my skull, a cruel reminder of my current predicament. The musty smell of hay filled my nostrils, mixing with the faint scent of something more repugnant in the corners of the barn. I blinked rapidly, trying to shake off the fog of confusion that clouded my mind.

With a grunt of effort, I leaned my back against the rough wooden wall, using it as leverage to push myself up to my feet. My wrists ached from the rough ropes binding me, the fibers cutting into my skin. I wobbled for a moment, the dizziness threatening to pull me back down, but I steadied myself, forcing my legs to hold my weight.

As I scanned the barn, the reality of my situation settled in. The floor was scattered with hay, much of it damp and clumped together, and in the dim light, I could see a few mice scurrying in the corners, their tiny bodies darting through the straw. It was surreal, almost absurd, to think that life continued on in this place despite the darkness that enveloped me. I felt an inexplicable connection to those little creatures—desperate, seeking shelter, yet trapped in a world that offered no safety.

My mind raced with questions. Where was I? How had I ended up here? I remembered the blow to my head, the darkness that had swallowed me whole, and now I was trapped in this barn, with no idea of how to escape. Panic clawed at my throat as I realized I had no weapon, no cellphone, no way to call for help. I was utterly alone.

I took a deep breath, forcing myself to focus. I needed to think. I had to find a way out. The ropes binding my wrists felt like chains, heavy and unyielding. I glanced around, searching for anything that could help me. The barn was dim, sunlight filtering through cracks in the wooden walls, but it felt like a tomb rather than a refuge.

My heart raced as I considered my options. I couldn't just sit here and wait for the Crow to come back. I had to escape. I had to find Natalie. The thought of her in danger sent a surge of adrenaline through me, sharpening my focus.

I shuffled toward the far wall, my feet crunching against the hay. I winced at the sound, fearing it would alert anyone nearby, but I was too desperate to care. I needed to find a weakness in my restraints, a way to loosen the ropes. I pressed my back against the wall, trying to find leverage.

As I struggled, the pain in my head intensified, but I pushed through it. I twisted my wrists, feeling for any give in the knots—anything that might offer me a chance. The ropes were rough against my skin, but I fought through the discomfort and kept twisting, gritting my teeth against the pain.

My head was pounding, and the pain made it hard to think straight. As I pressed my back against the barn's rough wooden wall, I felt the coolness of the wood seep through the thin fabric of my shirt, grounding me momentarily. I could see a few mice scurrying in the corners, and I couldn't help but wonder what was happening outside this prison of hay and shadows. I was utterly alone, and the weight of that isolation pressed down on my chest like an anvil.

Fear gripped me as I contemplated the reality of my situation. What if I never made it out of here? What if this was the end? The thought sent a chill through my bones, and I felt my breath quicken. I closed my eyes, trying to block out the impending dread, but it flooded in relentlessly.

I had dreams—dreams that felt so far out of reach now. I had always imagined my life unfolding in beautiful ways: marrying the love of my life, building a family filled with laughter and love, watching my children grow. The thought of walking my daughter down the aisle someday, of having that first dance with her—those moments now seemed like cruel taunts, shimmering just out of reach. Would I ever get to experience those things? Would I ever get to be a father?

The fear of dying consumed me, leaving me gasping for air as if the very thought could suffocate me. I envisioned the faces of those I loved, the joy of family gatherings, the warmth of shared moments. I could picture Natalie in a beautiful white dress, twirling in the sunlight, her laughter echoing in my ears. I could see her smile, her eyes sparkling with happiness. And then I imagined the silence that would follow if I were gone.

What would she think? Would she blame herself? The thought of her carrying that burden made my heart ache. I felt tears prick at the corners of my eyes, the frustration of my helplessness spilling over. What if I never got to tell her how much she meant to me? What if I never got to hold her close, to reassure her that everything would be okay?

I could feel the panic rising in my chest, a tidal wave of emotion that threatened to drown me. My vision blurred, and I struggled to keep my thoughts together. "No," I whispered to myself, forcing the words through gritted teeth. "I can't think like this. I have to stay strong."

But the fear kept creeping in, gnawing at the edges of my resolve. The Crow was out there, watching us, stalking us. How had he found us? How did he know we were at the park? I had been so focused on the conversation with Natalie, on the truths we were trying to unravel, that I hadn't even considered that someone might be watching.

I racked my brain, trying to remember—had I noticed anyone following her car? Had there been shadows lurking in the corners of my vision? My heart raced as I replayed the moments leading up to my abduction, searching for clues, but nothing felt concrete. It was all too weird, too terrifying. The Crow was a phantom in the night, a dark figure that seemed to know our every move.

What if he was someone I knew? The thought sent a jolt of fear through me, my mind spinning with possibilities. Who could he be? I felt trapped in a nightmare where every shadow held a threat, and every creak of the barn seemed to whisper my doom.

I took a deep breath, trying to anchor myself in the present. I had to focus. I had to escape this place, not just for myself but for Natalie. I couldn't let her down. I wouldn't let my fears dictate my fate. I had to find a way out, to fight back, to protect the future I desperately wanted.

But as the darkness pressed in around me, I couldn't shake the fear that maybe, just maybe, this was the end of my story.

I again struggled against the ropes, my hands burning from the friction, when I heard a noise—a sliding door creaking open. My heart raced as I froze, fear gripping me like a vice. *Who was it? Was it the Crow? Was he coming to finish what he started?*

CHAPTER 26

DOM

The barn door slid open with a creak that seemed to echo through the stillness, and my heart sank as Natalie walked in. Her face was blank, devoid of any emotion, as she moved toward me with a slow, deliberate pace. It was as if she were in a trance, a puppet on strings pulled by forces I couldn't comprehend.

"Natalie!" I called out, panic creeping into my voice. "What are you doing?"

She didn't respond, her eyes vacant, staring straight ahead as if she were walking through a dream. "Are you the one killing these people?" I pressed, desperation clawing at my throat. "What are you doing? Let me go!"

Without a word, Natalie began to pour gasoline around the barn, the flammable liquid glimmering ominously in the dim light. My heart dropped as the realization hit me like a punch to the gut—she was the Crow. All this time, it had been her. But why? Why would she kill people? It didn't make any sense.

"Natalie, please!" I shouted, trying to reach the girl I knew, the woman I loved. "You don't have to do this! We can get through this together!"

She continued to move around the barn like a zombie, her actions mechanical and devoid of the warmth that had once filled her. I felt a chill run down my spine. I didn't recognize this person. It was as if she had split into two entities: one that I loved and another that was a cold, ruthless killer.

I glanced around, searching for something—anything—that could help me escape this nightmare. In the far corner of the barn, I spotted an old saw, rusted and covered in dust. It was my only hope. I had to cut these ropes.

With every ounce of determination, I shifted my weight, trying to maneuver my body closer to the saw. She was still oblivious to me, moving with a single-minded focus as she continued to pour gasoline, creating a sinister trail around the perimeter of the barn. I could hear the liquid sloshing and pooling, and a sense of urgency gripped me.

Finally, after what felt like an eternity, I managed to reach the saw and pulled it close. My hands shook as I began sawing away at the ropes binding my wrists, the rough fibers biting into my skin. Time felt like it was slipping away, each second stretching into an eternity as I fought to free myself. I could smell the gasoline—sharp and acrid—filling the air, and the reality of what would happen if I failed sent a surge of adrenaline coursing through my veins.

The ropes finally broke, and I was free. I wasted no time, pushing myself to my feet. I felt the weight of the world on my shoulders as I faced the woman I loved, now an embodiment of darkness. I knew I had to bring her in, to save her from herself, even if it meant a fight to the death.

As I charged forward, I tackled her to the ground, the impact jarring my body. She fought back fiercely, headbutting me with a force that broke my nose. Pain exploded across my face, and I staggered back, blood spilling from my nostrils. But I couldn't give up.

I swung at her, my fist connecting with her face, but she barely flinched. It was as if she were made of stone, her eyes still cold and unyielding. In a split second, she grabbed me, flipping me over with a surprising strength. We landed on the ground in a tangle of limbs, both of us scrambling to regain control.

We were both in fighting positions now, staring each other down. I looked into her eyes, desperately searching for a hint of recognition, a flicker of the warmth and love that had once defined our relationship. But all I saw were cold, hollow depths—an abyss where the woman I loved had once resided.

"Natalie," I pleaded, my voice cracking. "Come back to me."

She tilted her head to the side, a strange, unsettling curiosity crossing her features before she charged at me with wild abandon. I sidestepped her, narrowly avoiding the collision, and in a split second, I grabbed her from behind, holding her tight. "Natalie, please! You don't have to do this!" I screamed into her ear, my heart breaking at the sight of her like this.

But there was no recognition in her eyes, only a primal rage that fueled her movements. With a surprising burst of strength, she broke free from my grip, spinning around to face me once more. I could see that the battle was not just physical; it was a deep struggle between the woman I knew and this dark persona that had taken over.

She lunged at me again, and instinct kicked in as I dodged to the side, narrowly avoiding her attempted grasp. The barn around us felt like a cage, the dim light casting eerie shadows that danced on the walls, making the situation feel all the more surreal. With each movement, I could hear the gasoline sloshing and pooling dangerously close to our feet, a ticking time bomb adding to the urgency of the fight.

"Natalie!" I shouted, my voice hoarse. "Fight it! You're stronger than this!"

But she didn't respond. Instead, she charged at me again, and this time, I braced myself. I sidestepped her attack and swept my leg out, knocking her off balance. She stumbled, but quickly regained her footing, her eyes filled with fury.

I was scared—scared of losing her, scared of what she had become. This was the hardest fight of my life, not just for my survival but for her soul. I had to reach her. I couldn't let this darkness consume her completely.

As she recovered, I saw a glimmer of something in her eyes—a flicker of doubt, perhaps. I seized the moment, stepping forward and grabbing her shoulders. "Natalie, listen to me!" I pleaded, my voice rising above the chaos around us. "You don't have to be the Crow! You don't have to kill!"

For a brief moment, I thought I saw a flicker of recognition, a spark that whispered of the woman I loved beneath the surface. But it vanished as quickly as it appeared, replaced by a fierce determination. She pushed me away, and I stumbled backwards, struggling to regain my balance.

"Why are you doing this?" I yelled, desperation creeping into my voice. "This isn't you! Fight it!"

With a primal scream, she lunged again, and I barely managed to dodge her. I could feel the adrenaline coursing through my veins, sharpening my senses as I fought to keep my head clear. I needed to find a way to subdue her, to bring her back from the brink.

We circled each other, the tension thick in the air. The barn felt like a battleground, the hay scattered beneath our feet, a stark reminder of the life we once shared and the darkness that now threatened to consume us.

Then, in a flash, she charged at me once more. I braced myself, and as she reached for me, I sidestepped, grabbing her arm and twisting it behind her back. She let out a cry of surprise and anger, but I held tight, my heart racing as I pressed my body against hers, trying to contain her fury.

"Please, Natalie!" I shouted, my voice breaking. "I love you! Come back to me!"

For a moment, she froze, and I felt the tension in her body waver. I could feel her breathing heavy against me, the warmth of her skin contrasting with the coldness in her eyes. "You're stronger than this," I urged, refusing to let go. "You can fight this!"

Suddenly, she twisted violently, breaking free from my grip and spinning around to face me. I had underestimated her resolve, and she lunged again, this time catching me off guard. I stumbled back, and before I could react, she tackled me to the ground, pinning me beneath her.

"You don't understand!" she screamed, her voice filled with a mix of rage and desperation. "You don't know what I've done!"

"I don't care what you've done!" I shouted, struggling beneath her weight. "I care about who you are! You're not a killer, Natalie!"

Her expression faltered for a split second, and I seized the opportunity. With all my strength, I rolled us over, now pinning her beneath me. I could see the confusion swirling in her eyes, and I knew I had to act fast.

"Natalie, please!" I begged, my voice raw with emotion. "You're still in there! Fight it! You're not this monster!"

As I held her down, I could feel the muscles in her body tense, the fight still raging within her. She thrashed against me, but I refused to let go. I wouldn't give up on her. I couldn't.

With every ounce of energy, I pressed my forehead against hers, locking my gaze onto her cold eyes. "Remember us," I whispered, the words spilling out like a prayer. "Remember who you are. You're stronger than this darkness. You can overcome it!"

CHAPTER 27

DOM

For a moment, silence enveloped us, the chaos of our struggle fading into the background. I could see the flicker of recognition in her eyes again, a glimmer of the love we once shared. "Dom..." she breathed, her voice barely above a whisper.

But before I could respond, the rage surged back, and she pushed me off with a fury that caught me off guard. I stumbled back, the world around me spinning as I tried to regain my footing.

"Natalie!" I shouted, my heart racing. "Please! You have to fight it!"

With a primal scream, she charged at me once more, and I braced myself for impact. But this time, something shifted in the air. The barn felt charged with electricity, an unspoken tension that hung between us like a storm ready to break. I had to believe there was still a part of her that could hear me, that could respond to my pleas.

As she lunged, I sidestepped, but this time I didn't just dodge her; I grabbed her wrist mid-attack, holding her arm tightly. I could feel the heat radiating from her skin, the wild energy coursing through her as she struggled against my grip. "Natalie!" I shouted, desperation flooding my voice. "Fight it! Please!"

Her face contorted with a mix of anger and confusion, and for a brief moment, I saw a flicker of the woman I loved —the warmth, the kindness that once lit up her eyes. "Dom..." she breathed again, voice trembling as if battling between two worlds—one filled with light and love, the other shrouded in darkness.

I tightened my grip, refusing to let go. "You're not a monster, Natalie! You're not the Crow! Remember who you are! Remember us!"

The fire in her eyes flickered, and I could see the internal struggle playing out like a violent storm. She twisted again, trying to break free, but I held on, my heart racing as I felt the ropes of her anger begin to unravel. "You're stronger than this!" I urged, my voice rising above the chaos. "You can fight it! You can choose to come back!"

She paused, her breath coming in ragged gasps. "I can't..." she whispered, tears welling in her eyes. "I've done terrible things, Dom. I can't go back."

"Everyone makes mistakes, Natalie! But you have the power to change! You have the power to choose!" I pressed, my heart aching for her. This was the hardest fight of my life —not just for my survival, but for her soul, for the love we had shared.

Suddenly, she lunged again, a wild, desperate motion fueled by fear and rage. I stumbled back, losing my grip on her wrist, and she darted toward the edge of the barn where the gasoline pooled ominously. My heart sank as I realized what she intended to do.

"No!" I shouted, adrenaline surging through me. I couldn't let her do this. I couldn't let her destroy herself. I charged after her, lunging forward just as she grabbed a match from her pocket, flicking it with a swift motion. The flame ignited, a bright, terrifying glow that illuminated her face and cast dark shadows across the barn.

She held the match close to the gasoline, the fire ready to consume everything in its path. "You don't understand!" she screamed, the wildness in her voice echoing off the barn walls. "This is the only way to end it!"

I reached her just in time, my hands grasping her wrist and forcing it down, the match nearly touching the flammable liquid. The flame flickered dangerously, and I felt the heat radiating off it. "Natalie, please! You don't have to do this!" I shouted, struggling to wrestle the match from her grip.

She fought back, her eyes wild with fear and desperation. "You don't know what I am! You don't know what I've done!"

"I know you're stronger than this!" I yelled, my voice raw with emotion. "You're not defined by your past! You can choose to walk away from this darkness!"

In that moment, I saw a flicker of doubt in her eyes, a crack in the armor she had built around herself. "Dom..." she whispered again, her voice breaking. "I don't want to hurt you."

"Then don't!" I cried, my heart pounding in my chest. "Let me help you! You're not alone in this!"

With a surge of determination, I yanked the match from her grasp and threw it to the ground. The flame extinguished before it could ignite the gasoline, and I felt a rush of relief wash over me. But the battle wasn't over yet.

Natalie recoiled, her expression shifting as she processed what had just happened. For a moment, it felt like we were suspended in time, the chaos of our surroundings fading into the background. I took a chance and stepped toward her, my heart in my throat.

"Natalie, I love you," I said softly, desperation lacing my voice. "Please, come back to me. You can fight this. You're not the Crow. You're not a killer. You're my Natalie."

She blinked, and I saw a glint of recognition in her eyes— a glimmer of the woman I had fallen in love with. But just as quickly, the darkness threatened to swallow her again. "No, Dom! I can't!" she cried, shaking her head violently as if trying to dispel the shadows.

"Yes, you can!" I urged, stepping closer. "You have the strength to overcome this. You're not alone. I'm here with you. Together, we can fight this!"

She shook her head again, and I could see the tears streaming down her face, mixing with the rage that had consumed her. "I've hurt people, Dom. I can't go back. I can't face what I've done."

"Then let me help you face it!" I pleaded, reaching out to touch her arm gently. "We can figure this out together. You don't have to carry this burden alone."

For a moment, everything hung in the balance. I could feel the energy shifting, the tension in the air thickening as I stared into her eyes, searching for any sign of hope. But just as I thought I had reached her, the darkness surged back, and she let out a low, guttural growl.

"No!" she screamed, her voice a mixture of pain and anger. "I won't let you in! I can't let you get hurt!"

Before I could react, she lunged at me again, and instinct kicked in. I sidestepped her attack, grabbing her from behind once more. "Natalie, please!" I shouted, holding her tightly, trying to contain the wild energy that threatened to consume her. "You're not a monster! You're my Natalie, and I refuse to let you go!"

She struggled against my hold, her body tense and rigid. I

felt her breath against my neck, hot and erratic. "You don't understand what I've done!" she cried, her voice breaking. "I can't go back! I can't let you see me like this!"

"I want to see you!" I shouted back, my heart racing. "I want to see the woman I love! I'm not afraid of your past. I'm here to fight for you!"

Then, unexpectedly, she stopped fighting. I felt her body go limp in my arms, and for a moment, I thought I had broken through the darkness. "Dom…" she whispered, her voice barely audible. "I'm so scared."

"I know," I said softly, my heart aching for her. "But we can face this together. You're not alone. You're stronger than you think."

As I held her close, I could feel the warmth of her body slowly returning—her essence seeping back through the cracks of despair that had overtaken her. I tilted her head back gently, forcing her to look into my eyes. "You can do this, Natalie. I believe in you."

For a heartbeat, it felt like we were suspended in a world of our own, the chaos of the barn fading away as the connection between us deepened. But just as I thought I had her back, the darkness surged again, and she pushed away from me, her eyes flashing with anger and fear.

"I can't!" she screamed, her voice echoing off the barn walls. "I don't know how to stop!"

"Natalie, listen to me!" I said, desperation clawing at my throat. "You're not a killer! You're not the Crow! You have the power to choose who you want to be!"

With a sudden burst of energy, she charged at me again, and I braced myself. This time, I sidestepped and grabbed her from behind, spinning her around. "Natalie!" I shouted, holding her tightly. "You have to fight this! You're stronger than this darkness!"

But she was relentless, struggling against my hold, her

breath coming in ragged gasps. I could feel the fear radiating off her, mingling with the fury that had taken root inside her. "Let me go!" she screamed, her voice filled with anguish.

"No!" I shouted back, holding her tighter. "I won't let you go! I won't let you become a monster!"

And then, in a moment of sheer desperation, I pressed my forehead against hers, trying to connect with the woman I loved. "Natalie, please! Come back to me! Fight this darkness! I love you!"

For a split second, her eyes softened, and I could see the flicker of recognition. "Dom..." she whispered, her voice breaking. "I don't want to hurt you."

"You won't," I promised, my heart racing. "I'm here with you. You can fight this. You're not alone."

But before I could react, she twisted away from me again, her eyes filled with a mix of rage and fear. The darkness surged within her, and I realized that this fight was far from over. I had to find a way to bring her back, to save her from the abyss that threatened to consume her completely.

As she lunged once more, I braced myself, ready for the fight of my life. This wasn't just about survival; it was about love, and I would do whatever it took to save her. I had to believe that somewhere beneath the layers of darkness, the woman I loved was still there, waiting for me to pull her back into the light. When finally whatever had a hold onto her let her go and her eyes changed back to normal.

"Dom, where are we?" Natalie's voice trembled, breaking through the heavy silence of the barn. Her brow furrowed with confusion, and her eyes darted around, taking in the dim light filtering through the cracks in the wooden walls. Shadows danced ominously in the corners, and the musty smell of hay filled the air, mixing with the faint, lingering scent of gasoline.

I forced a laugh, though it felt hollow in my throat. "We're in a barn right now," I replied, trying to keep my tone light, despite the fear that gripped my chest. The sight of her, disoriented and vulnerable, made my heart ache. She deserved to be safe, far away from the darkness that had brought us here.

"Why are you bleeding?" she asked, her voice filled with concern, her eyes locking onto the crimson streaks trailing down my face. I could feel the sting of my broken nose, the pain a stark reminder of the chaos we had just endured.

"Shaving," I coughed out, forcing a grin, but it did little to mask the reality of the situation. I could see the worry etched on her face, and I hated that I was the reason for it. "Let's get out of here, okay?" I urged, my voice steadier than I felt.

"Okay," she replied, her determination shining through the fear in her eyes. "My love, let me help you up."

As she reached for me, I felt the warmth of her hand against mine, grounding me in the midst of the turmoil swirling around us. I took a moment to absorb her presence, the way her red hair framed her face, the softness of her gaze that still held so much love despite the shadows that had threatened to consume us.

With her help, I slowly pulled myself to my feet, the world around me swaying like a ship on turbulent waters. My legs felt unsteady beneath me, every muscle aching from the struggle we had just endured. I could hear the creaking of the barn, the distant rustling of hay, and the faint scurrying of mice in the corners, all punctuating the eerie silence that surrounded us.

"Natalie," I said, my voice low and serious as I steadied myself, "we need to find a way out of here. We have to stay focused."

She nodded, her expression resolute. "I know," she said, her voice steady despite the chaos that had unfolded. "Together, we can do this."

As we took in our surroundings, the dim light revealed the splintered beams of wood above us, the hay scattered across the floor, and the ominous shadows lurking in the corners. I could feel the weight of the gasoline trailing dangerously close to where we stood, a reminder of the peril that still lingered.

"Where do you think the exit is?" Natalie asked, her voice a whisper as she scanned the barn.

"I'm not sure," I replied, my heart racing. "But we need to be careful. We can't let our guard down."

With each step, I felt the adrenaline coursing through my veins, pushing me forward despite the pain. I could see the determination in Natalie's eyes, a fire igniting within her that I hadn't seen in a while. It was a reminder of who she truly was beneath the darkness that had threatened to consume her.

"This way," I said, gesturing toward a door at the far end of the barn, partially obscured by shadows. As we moved cautiously, I could feel the tension in the air, the weight of the unknown pressing down on me. When the lights in the barn went out completely.

CHAPTER 28

DOM

"Dom, what is happening?" Natalies voice quivered, panic threading through her words. Her breath came in short gasps, and her eyes darted around the dimly lit barn, searching for something—anything—that could make sense of our horrifying reality. I could feel her fear, a palpable force that wrapped around us like a thick fog.

"I don't know, Nat," I replied, my voice steadier than I felt. My heart pounded in my chest, each beat echoing the urgency of the moment. I felt a cold sweat trickle down my back, the air in the barn thickening with an oppressive dread. "We need to stay calm. We'll figure this out."

But just as I finished speaking, a low, sinister laugh reverberated through the barn, echoing off the wooden walls and sending chills racing down my spine. The sound was distorted, twisted, as if it had been filtered through a dark, malevolent entity. I looked at Natalie, her eyes wide with terror, and I felt an icy grip around my heart.

"Did you hear that?" she whispered, her voice barely above a breath.

Before I could respond, a voice crackled to life, the sound emanating from an intercom hidden somewhere in the shadows. "Welcome, welcome!" it crooned, a mocking tone laced with malice. "How delightful to see you both awake. It's time for the show to begin."

The words wrapped around us like a noose, tightening with every syllable. I could feel the color drain from my face as the realization settled in. There was no escape. We were trapped in this nightmarish place, and whoever was behind the voice was reveling in our fear.

"What do you want from us?" I shouted, my voice echoing in the eerie silence that followed. My heart raced as the voice continued, unfazed by my challenge.

"Oh, but it's not what I want," it replied, dripping with sadistic pleasure. "It's what you'll do to survive."

Natalie clutched my arm, her grip tight and trembling. I could feel her body shaking beside me, and I fought against the rising tide of despair. "Dom, we have to get out of here!" she urged, her voice rising in pitch. "We can't let him—whatever he is—take us!"

"I know," I replied, trying to keep the panic from seeping into my voice. "We'll find a way. Just stay close to me."

I scanned the barn, my eyes darting from the shadows to the corners, searching for any sign of an exit. The dim light illuminated the hay scattered across the floor, casting long, flickering shadows that danced menacingly along the walls. The atmosphere was charged, heavy with the scent of musty hay and the lingering hint of gasoline.

"Look!" Natalie exclaimed, pointing toward a door at the far end of the barn. It was slightly ajar, a sliver of darkness beyond it that beckoned us. "We have to get to that door!"

Without thinking, I nodded and took her hand, our

fingers entwining as we moved toward the exit. But as we hurried forward, the voice on the intercom crackled to life again, sending a jolt of fear through me.

"Oh, but you won't make it that easily," it taunted, the laughter echoing through the barn like a malevolent specter. "The fun is just beginning!"

My heart raced as I felt the weight of its words. I glanced back at Natalie, her face pale, eyes wide with terror. "We can't let him get to us," I said, trying to sound brave. "We have to keep moving."

But before we could reach the door, a loud clang echoed through the barn, and the heavy sliding door slammed shut with a resounding thud, sealing our fate. The sound reverberated in the silence, a finality that sent shockwaves of panic coursing through us.

"No! No!" Natalie cried, pulling at the door, but it wouldn't budge. "We have to get out! Dom, please!"

"Natalie, stay calm!" I urged, my voice rising above the chaos. "We'll find another way!"

But deep down, I felt the cold tendrils of despair wrapping around my heart. The voice continued to taunt us, its laughter echoing like a twisted melody. "You're in my world now, my little playthings. The only way out is through the game I've prepared for you."

"What game?" I shouted, desperation creeping into my voice. "What do you want from us?"

"Oh, it's simple," the voice replied, dripping with malice. "You must face your deepest fears. Only then can you hope to escape. But be warned, not everyone makes it out alive."

A surge of adrenaline coursed through me, igniting a fire of determination within my chest. "We won't play your game!" I shouted defiantly, but my voice faltered as the weight of the situation bore down on me.

Natalie's grip tightened around my arm, and I could feel

her trembling beside me. "Dom, what if we don't survive this?" she whispered, her voice shaking. "What if we don't make it out?"

"Don't say that!" I replied, forcing my voice to remain steady. "We will escape. I promise." But as I spoke, doubt gnawed at the edges of my mind. Could I keep that promise?

As the oppressive silence settled in again, I could feel the tension escalating. The air crackled with energy, and I glanced around, desperate for any sign of hope. The barn was a labyrinth of shadows and uncertainty, each corner hiding potential dangers.

Suddenly, the intercom crackled again, and the voice spoke, its tone dripping with sadistic anticipation. "Let the game begin!"

A series of loud thuds resonated from the shadows, and I felt my heart race as figures began to emerge from the darkness—disfigured silhouettes that moved with unnatural speed. My breath caught in my throat as I realized we weren't alone.

"Natalie, run!" I shouted, adrenaline surging through me as I yanked her toward the far corner of the barn. We dashed through the maze of hay bales, our footsteps muffled by the soft straw, but the grotesque figures pursued us relentlessly, their laughter echoing in the darkness.

"Where do we go?" Natalie gasped, glancing over her shoulder as one of the figures lunged for us, its skeletal hands reaching out with ravenous intent.

"Over there!" I pointed to a stack of hay bales, hoping they might provide some cover. We ducked behind them, pressing our backs against the rough texture of the hay as we held our breath, listening to the sounds of our pursuers.

The laughter echoed around us, a cacophony of madness that made my skin crawl. "You can't hide forever!" the voice taunted, growing closer. "The game is about survival, and survival means facing your fears!"

My heart raced as I glanced at Natalie, her eyes wide with terror. "We can't let them find us," I whispered, my voice barely audible. "We have to stay quiet."

The air was thick with an oppressive silence, the kind that settled in your bones and made your heart race. I could feel the cold sweat trickling down my spine, pooling at the small of my back as I stood with Natalie. She was a pillar of strength, unwavering and resolute, ready to face whatever malevolence lurked in the shadows. But even her steadfastness could not shield me from the encroaching dread clawing at my insides.

The world around us felt distorted, reality bending under the weight of an unseen force. As I glanced over my shoulder, my heart stuttered and then raced as I caught sight of Natalie. She had always been quick-witted and resourceful, but in this moment, she seemed almost a ghost, her face pale and drawn tight with fear.

I motioned to her shoe, where I could see the outline of a gun concealed beneath the worn leather. "Natalie, your—"

Before I could finish, her hand shot down, fingers deftly extracting the weapon. She cocked it with a sharp, metallic click that echoed through the suffocating silence, a sound that felt like a death knell. My heart pounded in my chest, each beat a reminder of our impending doom.

We stood back to back, the weight of the world pressing down on us, waiting, breath held tight in our throats. The darkness around us felt alive, pulsating with a sinister energy, and I could almost hear it whispering our fates. The air crackled with tension, a prelude to the storm that was about to unleash itself upon us.

And then it came.

A voice slithered through the shadows, low and malevolent, wrapping around us like a serpent. "Burning by my hand is a privilege, and your soul will join the countless others in the hands of the crow." The words dripped with malice, each syllable a dagger that pierced the fragile veil of hope that had begun to form in my heart.

Fear gripped me like a vice. My breath quickened, each inhalation sharp and ragged as I tried to steady myself. The laughter that followed was a cacophony of cruelty, echoing in the hollow chambers of my mind. It reverberated through the darkness, a sound so twisted that it sent chills racing up my spine.

I could feel Natalie tense beside me, my muscles coiling like a spring, ready to unleash fury against whatever horror awaited us. But I was paralyzed, ensnared by the terror that wrapped around my heart like a constrictor snake. My eyes darted around, searching for the source of that horrible laughter, but the shadows only deepened, swallowing any semblance of light.

"Natalie," I said, my voice was steady despite the tremor inside me, "we need to stay sharp. Whatever this thing is, it's toying with us."

I could see the determination etched on her face, but it felt like a fragile façade. I could almost hear the whispers in the darkness, taunting me with visions of what lay ahead. Images of twisted faces, eyes hollow and hungry, danced in my mind, clawing at my sanity. My heart raced, pounding so loud in my ears that I was sure it would betray me, revealing my terror to the entity lurking just beyond our sight.

Then the shadows shifted, coiling and writhed like smoke given life. The voice returned, a sibilant hiss that felt like ice water poured over my soul. "You think you can escape? You think your feeble weapons can protect you from my wrath?" The laughter that followed was a symphony of madness, a sound that twisted my insides and threatened to unravel me completely.

I watched Natalie clutch her weapon, a cold I struggled to suppress the rising tide of panic.

I found a board and grabbed it like a bat. My fingers trembled as I tried to steady my aim, but the terror inside me was a storm, raging and chaotic.

"Stay focused," Natalie whispered, her voice barely above a breath. I could hear the crack in her composure, the way fear nibbled at the edges of her bravado. "We have to stick together."

I nodded, but the movement felt mechanical, as if I were a marionette on strings of dread. The darkness thickened, pressing in on us from all sides, and I could feel it crawling over my skin, the sensation almost sentient. I could taste the metallic tang of fear on my tongue, a bitter reminder that this was not just a nightmare but a grotesque reality.

CHAPTER 29

DOM

We search for loose boards fighting to get out of the barn when we can smell smoke and the barn is on fire. My fingers slid over the rough, splintered surface of the wood, searching for any sign of weakness, any loose board that would grant us escape. "We can't let this place go up in flames around us!"

The scent of charred wood and acrid smoke filled the air. My heart raced, pounding against my ribcage like a wild animal desperate to escape. The flames danced hungrily in the corners of the barn, flickering shadows painting grotesque images on the walls. I could hear the crackling of the fire, the whisper of the wind, and the frantic breaths of my best friend, Natalie, beside me.

She nodded, her wide eyes reflecting the orange glow of the fire. "I know, I know! Just... just give me a second!" Her own hands were trembling, and I could see fear etched into her features, but there was something else too—a flicker of recognition, a glimmer of something I couldn't quite place.

The barn creaked ominously above us, the heat rising, suffocating. I could feel the sweat trickling down my back, mixing with the fear and adrenaline coursing through my veins. I took a deep breath, forcing myself to remain calm. "Look for anything loose! We can't die here, Nat!"

Suddenly, a thick cloud of smoke rolled towards us, and I doubled over, coughing violently. My lungs burned, the air stung my eyes, and I felt panic rising within me, threatening to spill over. I glanced at Natalie, who was now bent over, gasping for breath, her face pale.

"Just a little more!" I urged, pressing my palms against the wood, feeling for any splinter that might give way. The flames crackled louder, licking hungrily at the beams above us, and the heat intensified. "We have to get out!"

Then, with a sharp crack, one of the boards finally gave way. A glimmer of hope surged through me as daylight poured into the barn, illuminating our escape route. "Here! I found it!" I yelled, pulling at the board with all my strength. The wood groaned, splintered further, and I could almost taste freedom.

"Natalie! We have to hurry!" I shouted, my voice strained and hoarse.

But just as I thought we might make it, the sound of a bell —a soft, chiming sound—cut through the chaos, freezing Natalie in place. It was strange and ethereal, a haunting melody that seemed to echo in the midst of the chaos. I turned to Natalie, but she stood there, still as a statue, her eyes glassy and distant.

"Natalie!" I screamed, panic flooding my voice. "Snap out of it! We need to go!"

And then, from the shadows of the barn, a figure emerged, stepping into the light with an unsettling calmness.

FLAMES OF THE CROWS BETRAYAL

It was her therapist Alicia, the one who had been trying to help Natalie for years. But there was something off about her —an unsettling smile stretched across her face, and her eyes gleamed with a manic intensity.

"There, there, my sweet," she cooed, her voice dripping with a sickly sweetness. "You are asleep. You won't remember any of this. Go get in the car."

The barn burned around us, flames licking at the ceiling, and the smoke thickened, swirling like a dark ghost. I coughed again, my vision blurring for a moment as I tried to comprehend the scene unfolding before me.

"I'm the Crow. Are you surprised? Do you happen to know what a group of crows is called you dumb cop? A murder. And there are many of us living inside of me."

She held the gun up to my face and laughed sinisterly as the flames grew hotter and the smoke began to overcome my breathing.

"Yes, breathe become one of my children." she laughed,

"Natalie!" I yelled again, desperate, but she remained frozen, entranced by her therapist's words. "Don't listen to her! She's lying! We need to get out!"

The therapist's smile widened, and she stepped closer, her eyes narrowing at me. "Oh, but she needs to listen. She needs to follow the path I've laid out for her. It's the only way."

I felt a chill creep up my spine, dread pooling in the pit of my stomach. "What have you done to her?" I demanded, my voice shaking with anger and fear. "You're not taking her anywhere!"

The therapist's laugh echoed through the barn, high-pitched and unsettling. "You think you can stop me? This is bigger than you can imagine. Natalie is special—she has a purpose, and it's time for her to fulfill it."

The flames danced wildly behind her, licking the darkened sky, casting an eerie glow over the twisted landscape.

The barn, once a sanctuary for hay and livestock, now crumbled under the weight of its own destruction, the wood crackling and popping like a cacophony of tortured screams. Ash fell like snow, coating the ground where we stood, a charred graveyard for memories long gone. My heart raced, pounding a frantic rhythm against my ribs, each beat a desperate plea for survival.

Alicia's face was a grotesque mask of madness, illuminated by the flickering light of the fire. Her eyes, once bright with innocence, now burned with an intensity that sent chills racing down my spine. They were hollow, devoid of empathy, reflecting nothing but a twisted satisfaction. Her lips curled into a smile that held no warmth, just the cold, sharp edges of a predator savoring the thrill of the hunt. The gun she held was steady, unwavering, aimed directly at my forehead, and with every moment, I felt the weight of impending doom pressing down upon me.

"When Natalie was brought to me for therapy because her mother left her... I chose her. To be my own," she spat, each word laced with venomous pride.

"But you tried to pry her away from me to make her remember, and that's why I put a failsafe in her mind. To keep her from remembering all of her terrible trauma. The molestation, the fighting her parents had done."

"And when her mother, who was supposed to love her chose to leave her, I just couldn't sit back. I killed her. She was one of my therapy patients, and I told her to get the kids and leave that home. But did she listen to me? No... so she had to die."

"I still remember when I first killed that dumb little boy who made fun of my clothes in school. I wasn't as wise as I am now but I ripped out his eyes like a crow and pushed him in a lake."

She licked her lips as she continued to walk around the

embers of the flames slowly catching the grass around us on fire.

"Oh... they found out it was me but I was a child and after juvenile jail I was free, free to change my name and be someone... someone respected like a therapist to help the sickos who didn't know they were sick."

Her voice echoed across the charred remains of the barn, blending with the crackling flames as if they were part of the same twisted symphony. I could hardly breathe as I tried to process the madness spilling from her lips. She was unhinged, a puppet master reveling in the chaos she had orchestrated. The fire danced behind her, a fitting backdrop to the horror she unleashed upon the world.

She paced back and forth, her boots crunching on the charred earth, the sound sending ripples of fear clawing through me. "The couple in the car, they asked me what to do —whether they should get married, run away, or stay home. I told them to listen to me and go home. They weren't ready. So when I found them packing to leave? They too had to be killed. How can a crow be a murder without a flock? They didn't listen, so now they are a part of me." Her laughter bubbled up, a discordant melody that pierced through the air, mingling with the crackling flames as if they were laughing along with her twisted delight.

"Why Natalie? Why would you let her search for you and not tell her that you were the sadistic one killing all of those people?" My voice trembled as I stood, driven by a primal urge to confront the nightmare standing before me. Each step I took felt like walking on shards of glass, every inch bringing me closer to the precipice of my own destruction. It was as if I could feel the heat of the flames licking at my back, urging me to retreat, but I couldn't; not now.

"Because you are a coward," I continued, the words

spilling out before I could stop them. "Afraid of jail and afraid for people to know that you need therapy."

"People that need therapy can't admit what is wrong with them," she shot back, her voice dripping with disdain. "I can fool. I was abandoned by both parents, left alone to raise myself. And that's when I saw it—a crow eating a rodent. It saw me and didn't fly off. It allowed me to eat what it was eating. I became its child. Every day it fed me. I am the crow, not by choice but because it chose me. Like I chose her."

"Natalie!" I screamed, lunging toward her, my heart racing. I shook her shoulders, desperate to break the spell. "Wake up! You're stronger than this!"

But she didn't move. The therapist continued her eerie monologue, her voice slicing through the chaos. "You should just give up now. You can't save her; she's already chosen."

"Chosen?" My voice was hoarse as I took a step back, the realization crashing over me like a wave. "Chosen for what? What are you planning?"

The flames roared louder, the heat becoming unbearable. I could feel my skin prickling, and the smoke was suffocating. I had to act. I had to save Natalie. "Baby I love you with everything I am, if you can hear me, you are my very breath, everything I have ever needed or wanted. I love you and no matter what happens my heart will always be with you." I grabbed her lifeless face and placed my lips on hers before wrapping my arms around her for possibly the last time.

The therapist tilted her head, a twisted smile blooming across her lips. "Oh she can't hear you, you'll soon be a part of me."

"Never! My heart belongs to Natalie, not you, you evil witch!" I roared.

Her eyes flickered with a wild light, and I could see the shadows of her past swirling behind them—dark memories that twisted and turned, clawing at the remnants of her humanity. The flames illuminated her face, making her look like a demon risen from the depths of hell, her wickedness laid bare against the backdrop of destruction.

"You're sick," I whispered, the realization hitting me like a punch to the gut. My fear morphed into a sickening blend of pity and horror. This was a woman who had once held the lives of so many in her hands, and now she stood here, a twisted puppet master in a world of chaos she had created.

As the fire blazed higher, I could feel the heat engulfing me, matching the fury in her eyes. "You're nothing but a murderer,Alicia! You think you're a crow, but you're just a monster!"

Her laughter rang out again, echoing through the night, mingling with the crackling fire and the distant wails of the past. In that moment, I knew—this was not just the climax of our confrontation, but the apex of her twisted existence.

And then, in an instant, everything changed. My heart stopped, and the world around me faded into a blur of orange and black.

With a loud bang, the sound of the gunshot deafened my ears, and I felt a sudden, sharp pain in my chest. My legs gave way, and I crumpled to the ground, the heat of the flames licking at my skin.

But there was nothing. No pain, no fear—just silence.

CHAPTER 30

NATALIE

I woke up to the soft rays of sunlight filtering through the curtains, casting a warm glow across my bedroom. The world felt unreal, as if I was still trapped in a dream. I blinked, trying to shake off the remnants of sleep, only to feel an unsettling emptiness beside me. My heart raced as I turned to the other side of the bed, expecting to see him there, his chest rising and falling in a gentle rhythm. But the sheets were cold, and the space beside me was achingly empty.

I sat up, my heart pounding in my chest. The room felt foreign, as if I had entered a different life overnight. My eyes scanned the room, and that's when I saw it—a note, resting on the pillow with an engagement ring glinting under the morning light, a cruel reminder of promises made and now broken.

My hands trembled as I reached for the note, my breath

hitching in my throat. With shaking fingers, I unfolded the paper, the words blurring as tears threatened to spill.

"I'm sorry. I can't do this anymore. I hope you find someone who can love you the way you deserve. Please understand."

Mackinzie and Dad had gone back to her apartment to plan for my mothers funeral and here I was all alone... Dom, the one person I thought would never give up on me, had left me... *how was I going to find the crow now? Without my partner, my lover, my friend.*

Each word sliced through me like a knife, sharp and unforgiving. I felt the weight of despair crash over me, pulling me down into a dark abyss. The ring, once a symbol of love and commitment, now felt like a noose around my neck. I dropped the note and ring to the floor, unable to hold back the flood of emotions that surged through me.

"No, no, no!" I screamed, the sound echoing in the silence of the house. "This can't be happening!" My voice cracked, raw with anguish. I stumbled out of bed, my mind racing, searching for something, anything that would make this all feel real again.

But the truth was suffocating. He was gone. The life we had built together, the dreams we had shared, all reduced to a few cruel lines on a page. I felt the walls closing in around me as panic set in, a tight grip around my chest that made it hard to breathe.

I could hear his voice in my head almost like he was here with me. ***Baby, I love you with everything I am. If you can hear me, you are my very breath, everything I have ever needed or wanted. I love you and no matter what happens my heart will always be with you.***

But he wasn't with me at all. My mind was playing a cruel trick. I bitterly thought to myself, *"He didnt love me after all. He never did!"*

MIKEL WILSON

I tore through the house, my heart racing with each passing second. I could feel the anger bubbling inside me, a fierce, burning rage that begged to be released. I flung open drawers, sending clothes and belongings flying across the room. I smashed picture frames against the wall, shattering glass and memories alike. The laughter we shared, the moments captured in those pictures—they felt like a betrayal now, mocking me with their permanence while everything else crumbled into dust.

The chaos of my destruction mirrored the turmoil in my heart. I was a whirlwind of emotions, caught between anger and despair, and I didn't know how to stop. I wanted to scream, to cry, to unleash the pain that threatened to consume me.

Finally, I collapsed on the floor, my body sliding down the wall as I gasped for breath. I pulled my knees to my chest, wrapping my arms around them as if trying to hold myself together. I could feel the panic attack rising within me, a tide of fear and despair that threatened to drown me.

"Please," I whispered, my voice barely audible. "I can't do this. I can't live like this."

The weight of it all was too much. I wished for death, for an escape from the suffocating pain that wrapped around me like a vice. My heart ached, a hollow pit that echoed with the memories of his laughter, his touch, the warmth of his presence that now felt like a ghost haunting the empty spaces of our home.

I fumbled for my phone, my fingers shaking as I dialed my therapist's number, praying for a lifeline, a way to claw my way back from the edge. The phone rang, each tone a reminder of my desperation.

"Hello?" My therapist's voice broke through the fog of my despair, calm and steady, a beacon in the storm.

"Please," I gasped, tears streaming down my face. "I need help. He's gone. He left me. I can't breathe. I can't—"

"Breathe," she said softly. "In and out. Just focus on that. I'm here. You're safe."

Her voice was a lifeline, grounding me amidst the chaos. I tried to follow her instructions, to breathe, but each inhale felt like a jagged shard of glass scraping my throat. I was falling apart, and I didn't know how to stop it.

"Can you tell me where you are?" she asked, her tone soothing, coaxing me back from the edge.

"I'm... I'm at home," I stammered, my voice breaking. "I don't know what to do. He was everything. I thought we were going to get married. I thought..." My words trailed off into a sob, the pain crashing over me in waves.

"It's okay to feel this way," she said gently. "You're grieving a loss, and that's valid. It's going to hurt, but you're not alone in this. I'm here. Let's take it one step at a time."

With each word, I felt the edges of my despair begin to soften, just a little. I still felt lost, but there was a flicker of hope buried beneath the rubble of my heart. I closed my eyes, focusing on her voice, trying to latch onto it like a lifeline in the stormy sea of my emotions.

"Can you tell me about him?" she prompted, and I felt a fresh wave of tears spill down my cheeks.

I took a shaky breath, my heart aching at the memories. "He had this way of making everything feel right. He would hold me when I had bad days, and he always knew how to make me laugh. I thought we had a future together. We talked about kids, about building a life..."

But now it felt like a cruel joke, a dream that had evaporated into thin air. I could hardly bear the weight of it all.

"Those memories are beautiful," my therapist said, her tone steady. "But it's okay to be angry, too. It's okay to feel betrayed. He made a choice that hurt you, and you deserve to feel that pain."

I nodded, the tears falling faster now, pooling on the floor beneath me. The anger swirled within, a tempest fighting against the overwhelming sadness. "I just... I don't understand why. Why would he leave? Did I do something wrong? Was I not enough?"

"No," she said firmly. "You are more than enough. His choice reflects his struggles, not your worth. You deserve love and respect, and you will find that again, even if it feels impossible right now."

The thought of moving on felt like a distant dream, yet her words wrapped around me like a warm embrace, soothing the jagged edges of my heart.

We talked for what felt like hours, the panic slowly receding as she guided me through my thoughts and feelings. I still felt broken, but through the tears and the heavy weight in my chest, I sensed a flicker of something—hope, perhaps? The storm within me began to quiet, if only just a little.

"Drive over and come sit with me in the office," she suggested gently. "I will help you through this."

Her voice wrapped around me like a warm blanket, soothing the frayed edges of my mind. I felt a spark of determination rise within me, a small but fierce desire to take back control. "Okay," I whispered, my voice still shaky.

"I'll be waiting," she reassured me.

I climbed into my car, my heart pounding not just with sorrow but with a burgeoning sense of resolve. The drive felt surreal; each turn and stop light blurred as I concentrated on her calming words. "Breathe, Natalie. You're going to be okay," I murmured to myself.

When I finally arrived at her office, the familiar exterior felt strangely comforting. I walked in, the soft chime of the doorbell signaling my entrance. The room smelled of lavender and freshly brewed tea—a stark contrast to the chaos in my mind. I took a deep breath, hoping to absorb some of that calmness.

"Hello, Natalie," my therapist said with a warm smile, gesturing for me to take a seat. "It's going to be okay. Just lean back and breathe. You have to calm your breathing."

I nodded, feeling the weight of her gaze on me, steady and reassuring. As I sank into the plush chair, I felt the tension in my shoulders begin to ease, if only slightly. "I don't know how to breathe," I admitted, my voice cracking as I fought against the rising tide of emotions.

"Let's take it slow," she said softly, her voice a gentle guide through the storm. "Start by inhaling deeply through your nose. Count to four as you breathe in."

I closed my eyes, focusing on her voice and the rhythm she set. I inhaled through my nose, counting silently, and felt my lungs expand. "One… two… three… four."

"Good," she encouraged. "Now hold that breath for a moment. Just feel it fill you up."

I could feel the air settling within me, a brief moment of fullness before the heaviness returned. "Now, exhale slowly through your mouth," she instructed. "Count to six as you let it all out. Ready?"

I nodded again, though my heart was still racing. "Okay. One… two… three… four… five… six."

With each exhale, I felt a little more of the tension slip away. It was as if I were releasing the fear and doubt that clung to me, even if just for a moment. "That's it, Natalie. Just keep breathing like that," she said, her voice a steady lighthouse guiding me through the fog.

As I continued this cycle of breaths, I focused on the sensation of the air filling my lungs and the subsequent release. The world outside faded, and in that moment, it was

MIKEL WILSON

just me and her, two souls in a room filled with understanding.

"Now, let's visualize something calming," she suggested. "Picture a place where you feel safe and at peace. It could be a beach, a forest, or even your favorite room in your house."

I concentrated, trying to conjure an image, but my mind was a whirlwind of memories and fears. "I don't know," I confessed, frustration creeping back in. "Everything feels tainted now."

"That's okay," she replied, her tone soothing. "Let's try something different. How about we work with what you're feeling right now? What's the first thing that comes to mind? What do you see?"

I took another deep breath, attempting to ground myself. "I see... darkness," I admitted, my voice barely above a whisper. "I feel trapped, like I can't escape."

"Good," she said, her voice steady and reassuring. "Acknowledge that darkness. It's there, but it doesn't define you. It's just a part of this moment. Now, think about what you would see if that darkness started to fade. What would be on the other side?"

"I don't know, I can't see anything. There's nothing there."

"Focus, do you see anything at all?" She asked.

EPILOGUE

NATALIE

*T*ears flowed down my face as I clutched the engagement ring box in my trembling hands. The cold metal felt like a dagger against my skin, a cruel reminder of the love I thought I had possessed for so long. "I can't believe he left me," I sobbed, pouring out my heart to my therapist, who listened with an understanding gaze.

"Maybe being a detective is too much stress on you. Have you thought of a career change?" she suggested gently.

"Like what, Dr. Alicia?" I asked, my voice cracking between the sobs. The thought of abandoning the only career I had ever known felt unfathomable, but there was no clarity amid the fog of despair.

. . .

MIKEL WILSON

SHE SMILED SUBTLY, her eyes glinting with an intensity I hadn't noticed before. "Perhaps something less demanding… something more fulfilling."

BEFORE I COULD RESPOND, she reached into her desk drawer and pulled out a small, ornate bell. My brow furrowed in confusion as she held it up, the light catching the polished surface. "What is that for?" I asked, anxiety slowly creeping back in. The hairs on my arm stood straight up. *What was this feeling? I couldn't place my finger on it.*

WITH A CALMNESS that sent a shiver up my spine, she rang the bell. The sound reverberated in the room, sharp and clear and then everything went dark and silent.

THE END

Betrayal doesn't come from a stranger or someone you barely know; betrayal comes from someone you trust.

Printed in the USA
CPSIA information can be obtained
at www.ICGtesting.com
CBHW051154181024
16013CB00007B/123